Plight of the Super Bee

by

Mackenzie Lloyd

It was a beautiful beginning. The sky was pale grey, as it often is in the early morning, which transitioned down as if it were blended by the hand of a skilled painter towards the lifeless empty white that sat just above the hued amber light of the sun as it began to illuminate the world from its hidden station. The clouds, though faintly seen, in an early start, were light and high in the sky; simply innocuously scrolling by. The limp leaves of the trees in the yards that measured the small towns rows of houses waited for rain. Along the silent street they pressed despairingly in the wind that forced upon them. To them, April had been most especially cruel; as the winter melted away revealing the deadness of everything; once the spring water dried it was hot and arid ever since. The uncomfortable feeling in the air beckoned change. Everything that breathed longed for a heavenly deluge. And luckily, to those keen to sense it, too much wind in the morning was not only a mild reprieve from heat, but a sign of weather to come; the growing pink sky in the morning was another thing. However, days had come and gone in spring with promise and no rain. But regardless of the weather, there slept, to some, a perfect little street in a perfectly still neighbourhood. There was a power-walking lady; an old man walking his dog; a solemn highschooler trudging out early to wait for a bus. To some, it was a perfect place. To others, there was only a dry wind pressing struggling leaves and dry grass.

In that early grey glow a quaint garage sat at the back of a driveway to the side and behind a small war-time bungalow that was ordinary to the street. A small, square, story-and-a-half, which had been pridefully owned at one time, currently sat in a state of unflattering antiquation.

Up the asphalt driveway, of which the weeds had found their way through the cracks and nestled within them and were enjoying a healthy and unbothered life, could be seen an open double-wide garage door. Within the depth of that dirty and poorly lighted place could be heard on a number of occasions the unmistakable sound of a box-end wrench clanging to a concrete floor, ringing out as a tuning fork sings, and a pair of ragged boot heels scuffling against a floor of an otherwise silent garage. From the opening of the large door peered out, the way some wild and barbarous beast looks out a zoo cage to the world that looks back at it, a set of intimidating glass eyes.

The boots protruded out from under the machine with the headlights that looked like a beast's eyes, while the half-hidden torso toiled under it. The garage was quiet except for those failed grasps of wrenches, shuffling of boot heels on a dusty concrete floor and occasional mummering of lamentations coming from a concealed place. The quiet commotion from within the garage was growing in harmony with the bloom of the morning of the outside world around it.

It was in the quiet stilled air of that detached little building that the owner of the ragged boot heels scuttled out from underneath his machine. Sliding his back across a sheet of cardboard (standard issue hot-rodder's equipment; creepers were for Bruce Springsteen music videos; they never got low enough to let one slide underneath much of anything, mention nothing of the cracks and pebbles that would infuriatingly stop them in their tracks) he stood erect and stepped back from his work and rested against a workbench. The young man looked in totality of the thing that he had, over a great amount of time, brought back from the dead, and leaned in admiration of it as he often did.

The black vinyl top was beautifully redone and a point of pride. Down the sides its forest green metallic flake complexion reflected a mysterious other world as when a still pool in a still place is peered into. Crager rims, BF Goodrich T/A Radial tires with raised white lettering, which were a bit out of vogue, but its owner didn't care he liked them, completed the curb appeal. Traversing the decklid was a subtle black tail-stripe which was difficult to see against the dark green colour. Inside were black leather bench seats; contrasting green trim including the large green, sun-cracked dash; a white-knobbed Hurst shifter, preferred from the pistol-grip style, protruded from the center of the floor and a partially sagging headliner which had, over time, transitioned to a disgusting grey. All-in-all, it was alright. It had come a long way to get how it was now. Though it was far from a trailer queen, and at most an unreliable driver, its novelty and rarity were its prevailing qualities.

It was a malleable and ethereal thing. It was what it was; it could be hammered into one box or label with a little work if one could be so inclined to do so; but mostly people knew it as it was. At times it was a forgotten or throw-away thought. Other times the unflinching bedrock at the foundation of someone's character. It was a theology embodied; the spirit of a nation materialized. However the world may change around it, though, the thing only exists as it does today. And what that exactly was might depend on who you ask.

To the front of the thing now, and with no true intention other than to maybe admire it more, there was an assertive pop given to the heavy steel hood as the latch was pulled and the whole thing predictably creaked up as it was raised. After a few moments of milling and mulling, poking and jiggling (accomplishing much of nothing); after the titillation of the initial sight of the thing's great heart, a familiar thought crept into the mind of its prodder and his temperament changed from broody pensiveness to being slightly sullen as he saw through the machine and lamented on its essence as he unwillingly did from time to time. Looking down to the skeleton of its being, he saw a thousand simple machines working more or less in unison. An old and familiar thought he'd often mull over. Not that he had anything against simple machines; how could one have contempt for the backbone of all industrial creation? But here that was all there was, and maybe, here under this hood, were all the wrong ones. A collaborative clunking, sputtering loud, undesirable mess when in the wrong mood. The machinations of the prosperous fed by the spoils of unseen turmoil, toiled on by greasy hands and ignorant minds. That's what he thought anyway; *might be a bit cynical..* But ignorance is bliss and as he shook off those thoughts, thought instead of how it was a hell of a cool car.

Under the hood, and all things considered, it had a good engine. A three-hundred-eighty-three cubic inch power-plant from a 1970 Charger SE; or at least so says the serial number on the block if one could trust what the internet says. After about a decade of service in that Charger, through an anecdote of the previous owner, the still-beating heart, untimely ripp'd, was put into a d100 from which the year of that was unknown. Another decade of service passed followed by another of rest in a forgotten corner of some quiet garage until it was finally acquired by its current owner. After a bit more rest and eventual love and attention it now lay before him in this car that laid motionless here. It had 906 heads thanks to that Charger. And, thanks to one or more of the previous owners it also had a Edlebrock dual plane aluminum intake, a mild cam, headers and a Holley 3310, which was a 750cfm single pump with vacuum secondaries. Everything else was stock or superglue.

It was an engine rich in untold history. One that fought in the trenches so to speak; knee deep in salt marshes heaving a cutlass; slugging it out with challengers, come as they may, in unsanctioned street races in chest-beating displays of aggression at traffic lights; or some romantic notion of that. It was the smallest of the Chrysler big blocks. Capable yet attainable for your poor-man's-Richard Petty. Though the car was certainly no Petty car. It was far from any baby-blue GTX, nor was it an R/T or Hemi car for that matter. The car that this engine sat in was the car that just wasn't. A 1970 Dodge Coronet. The one year production run in that body style and a low trim level to boot. It had everything in place for that car to be great: pinnacle performance power in a Wild West time of engine development; uninhibited by fuel and emission sanctions of the early 70's, brash looks just-on-this-side-of gaudy that epitomized the short-lived golden age of those eccentric beasts and even it's own kitschy hook (for that of the older brother, the Super Bee), again, at the height of an era full of questionably absurd marketing gimmicks. An exciting frontier in personal transportation. An age of independence, liberty and innovation raging blindly into undiscovered country.

The young man that had been aimlessly poking and pulling and inspecting in the engine bay had finished and now set to aimlessly pacing back and forth across the empty space in the garage. Inside the garage was dark but out the large open door the sun was coming up for air, which provided the dim and lowly lit space with a pale colouring to everything inside as it waited for the Divine amber glow to come down and illuminate it. But right now it was a ghostly purgatory of inaction; an absolute still place when the pacer would halt still. At times, the only movement seemed to be the dancing particulation of the floating dust in the air as it hit the new light of day. It was a typical garage. It smelled as a garage should smell: a sharp smell; alien and toxic, even to those familiar to it, underlaid by a foundation of earthy musk and a faint trace of sweetness which came from the now-and-again grinding and melting of metal.

As the unattended sun rose, this Shangri-la-to-some came more and more into focus and the paleness of everything began to bloom into the true colours of themselves. It was ordinary to most people, indeed, but it was a place where Nirvana, on occasion, occurred in some folk. And as the light began to breathe life into that space and more and more things began to animate, the pacing halted and a drill press was used here or an area was organized there. The outside world's burgeoning brightness unveiling the radiance of the dawn was being regarded all along from behind the threshold of the great garage door opening; casually, as one leans against a post or loafs to and fro from garage end to end; props oneself against table or car and reflects on those things that stir in that world beyond that great opening. This was all before coffee, of course, of which there was a mug cooling on the workbench.

There was no milk in the house so the coffee this morning was black. The mug was cooling quickly so it was drunk fast in order to retain a shred of pleasantness. As it was sipped, the cacophony of the outside world began as an orchestra warms up before a performance. An early morning cube van clanked by; two women were jogging in tandem; the flash of two jet-like finches darted past; two cars drove by: a young professional looking girl in a small white Mitsubishi and then a young man in a jacked up truck; an overzealous squirrel made his presence known to the world as he wrestled with the fruits of a weekday morning.

The girl was cute and he pondered where she was off to; what her career was; and what the musings of her day would bring. He also pondered if she lived close by. He suspected that she must not've as he hadn't seen her around before. So she had spent the night at her boyfriend's place, he figured. Maybe her parents' house. *Apartment, maybe?* He didn't think there were many around there. A room in a house, maybe. He then thought that he might have known the boy. That was probably the boyfriend. But seeing as the girl looked to be a few years younger than he was, he decided that he might be aware of him but not know him all that well. That Mitsubishi she was driving was a small four door hatch or whatever you call them. She was using all of the four cylinders as she went just screaming by. She was hard on it. That, there was no doubt. Some people could break an anvil if you let them

Not to sound too *Holier-than-thou*, this young man knew, but there is a certain awareness one gets for mechanicians of things, in particular, when one is forced to change his own doing or undoing. When knuckles are wrapped and scraped on seized calipers; deteriorated ball joints; disintegrated bearings and all else that has become a mush of rubber and worn steel. Why anyone would toil with the detritus of any of it is a fine question; but some people must.

The young man's shoulder held up the garage as he stared peacefully out the aperture of the open door and drank his coffee as he took in the full morning trill. Thoughts shifted from the young woman in the car, to the two joggers, to the weather for the day and finally back once more to the joggers. They were older women in obviously remarkable shape. Their tight athletic wear left nothing to the imagination, yet simultaneously let the imagination spasm into a nebula of outrageous possibilities. He watched them trot in tandem as two mustangs might lope together over a rolling hill, and tried to put in an elegant way how they should stop for a moment and chat and after salutations and fervent flirtations. But he watched them pass in their tight athletic wear. And he didn't mind seeing them cross and descend the even slighter decline of the road to the east, underneath the large white oaks that lined the boulevard, dodging potholes as they ran. *What were they chasing*, he wondered? *Were they training for a marathon? Doubtful*, he thought. *Keeping up for their husbands? Or ooglers in grocery stores or at gas station pumps or wandering eyes in garage door openings? What prize were they after? What banner were they chasing?* If they stopped to talk, or if he met them one afternoon in a park, *what would they discuss? People, events; art? Would they speak of Michelangelo? I don't know.* It was a silly trail of thought to continue on. Maybe he'd think up something crazy about Lead-foot in the Mitsubishi; but she was in too much of a rush to care about anything, it seemed. He was about at his limit for that type, anyway.

With the street again quiet he watched the wind blow harder in the trees. Back and forth it blew, tossing the limbs to and fro. He watched the brilliant pink and orange sky behind those trees. A pink sky in morning; something for which he was not ready for.

This car needed to be buttoned up. It ran; the motor ran like a top (at last); it even made it around the block and down a street a bit before the bad vibrations from the driveshaft shut down a brief moment of euphoria. Something was wrong with that driveshaft and whatever it was shook the entire operation like a space shuttle on atmospheric re-entry. It was either completely toast u-joints or a balance weight had been knocked off or the thing was somehow bent. It could also be something wrong in the back end which was a dreadful notion. At any rate it really didn't matter as there was a new driveshaft sitting on the floor in front of the workbench that was about to be swapped in. The brakes also needed to be bled but that wouldn't (or shouldn't) take long.

He looked at his phone; *that fucking phone*. That small piece of thing that created so much grief to him. It was like a hot coal he was burdened to carry around. He knew it wasn't the phone itself and he was deferring a great deal of stress onto this inanimate thing, but it helped him if he thought about the phone in that way; being the genesis of his troubles. The phone was just like the car; that was just like the house; that was just like his family and his job... he looked at all the clutter on the work table. Empty and half empty cans of brake cleaner, rags, parts of parts and tools left little of the table itself visible. He scanned its surface, past another empty coffee mug, with its dried coffee running down the side, its remanence left in an unexpected essence to dry from the elements of the world. He saw another mug from the day before, and another on a shelf above from the day before that. In each of those a spoon; yes, he could measure out his life with coffee spoons. Except, now that the milk's run out, there is no more need for spoons. He felt the way an old dog must feel laying on a rug on the floor; deflated of vitality. He just wanted to lay on a floor somewhere in the sun beaming in from a window somewhere and be left alone. He made the decision that he should probably take the mugs into the house at some point soon. Although, what he was really in the middle of was looking for a tool. And though his "organization" was spread out in bedlam throughout the table, and in a grander respect to the rest of the garage, he had a sense of where everything was (most of the time). He looked at his phone lying there: motionless; inanimate; dark. His smile fell heavily among the bric-a-brac. He looked at the infernal mess of rust, filings, nuts, bolts, spanners, hammers and ratchet-drills. Things he loved, because he got on with them. But that morning on that table no thing gleamed. His phone sat there and he just stared at it and it was dark.

He forgot about his phone for now and let it rest there on the workbench. He located the tools he was looking for and prepared himself to get down and slide himself under the car which was propped up on jack stands at all four corners. He needed to swap the driveshaft. So he creaked and groaned down on that corrugated cardboard on the floor and once more he scuttled and shimmied underneath the crusted cake of the underbody. He did his work and freed it up and then slipped it back off the splined shaft only after a few more trips out from under the car to grab a pry bar or a can of penetrant and a butane torch and finally back again; that's how it goes. He tossed it to the side with a dismissive clank as it fell. Then he laid on his back for a while; his arms laid out to each side; palms up and he just laid there. After a while he'd kick that shaft out to the side and slide out from underneath and get the new (well, "new") shaft and do the whole thing over again in reverse. He'd gotten a good deal on a used one so he took a bit of a chance of it being ok. He didn't have much to lose with this new shaft.

On one of his increasingly laborious trips down and under the machine he noticed a small puddle developing towards the front. *Probably coolant*, he thought to himself. A periodic...drip. One... had to ...watch. One had to watch for some time, as it was slow and imperceptible to an impatient observer. But with a slow maddening rhythm of a Friday afternoon clock it dripped into a fairly concerning puddle on the rough concrete floor under the front of the car. He'd check it out in a minute after he put some tools away. The driveshaft procedure went surprisingly well. It was in similar condition as the one that got removed but it came with assurance that it would fit this application and there weren't any problems with it, for whatever the going rate of a guy's word is these days. But for the money it cost, that was good enough to go through the effort. Time would tell if it was truly true. He'd go for a little drive later that day. But it did fit, at least; it was on there now. And now, with that task complete, full attention could be given towards the genesis of that puddle. He was relieved that at least something had gone swimmingly today.

The puddle steadily grew by a drop at a time. He heard his phone vibrate from the workbench two times. But, as he was on the ground eeking towards the front of the car, he ignored it for now. With each inching eek toward the drip his suspicions that it was a coolant leak were eventually confirmed. He investigated from which, where and why, and in short order discovered that it was coming from the lower rad hose where the clamp had rusted and given up its duty. Prodding further to see if its life could be extended by a slight readjustment he grabbed the hose and clamp and gave it a jiggle. In that instant the clamp gave it up entirely, popping the hose loose and sending a torrent of vile slime crashing down upon his face. Frantically, he tried to get the hose on the radiator again.

Though limited by space and factored by time, he struggled. The coolant got in his eyes and mouth and nose and it was impossible to see and with still such volume coming down the closer the hose got to fitting on the more violent the rain came. It was slightly sweet on the tip of his tongue and incredibly bitter throughout the rest of his mouth, it was sticky in his hair and on his skin; it burned his eyes. Eventually he had success, with the use of his mind's-eye a deliberate forceful shove of the hose back onto the fitting. After, he just laid there; prone; with a tenacious drip, twice the rate as before, dripping steadily beside him. He lay there, sticky; smelling the smell and tasting the poisonous bitter taste that had reached far in his nose, throughout his mouth and made his throat itch and burn.

His blood boiled as he lay there, but there wasn't much he could do at this point. The damage was done. Quelling his first instinct which was to get out from under the car in a panic, he calmed himself as best he could once the maelstrom ceased. He just laid where he was in that cold rancid rain; the cold unempathetic drip insulting him with splatter from each persisting drip. He thought about that infernal machine; that compilation of a thousand simple mechanisms, each as simple as its fellow counterpart; no one greater than the other. A thousand simple ideas working more or less in unison. *Old ideas.* He thought about the hundreds years of development and how many people worked collectively to perpetuate the same tired ideas; perfecting an imperfect thing. He slid out from underneath and raised with some difficulty. *You could shed a few, you know? Maybe twenty sit-ups later. Get back on a routine,* he lamented as he now just leaned there, breathing.

A thing whose every tentacle of being, from inception through service, extends maliciously into the earth and those that live on it. The American dream: from willing hands they grasp the torch, without question or introspection; but a primal desire for bigger, better, faster and more of it. Nothing has changed for a hundred years. This car was fast - one of the fastest. It was all the same from underneath, though; all of them.

The hood was still up on the car and again he found himself staring at the engine. And among the multitude of things that were flying through his mind one of them was that this giant block of iron was still relevant today. Still popular and desired even. He wanted to rip this thing out and push this huge hunk of ore, that had been hoarded for so long, down the street until he bumped into the first person that he met and give it to them. Why do you hoard such things, they'd say? Some people don't understand. Get a Prius, they'd scoff, and impose their consumerism. Well, there are a few theories on that; total carbon footprints and what-not; and then he would scoff. Maybe the philosophical jousting (all of which was an argument in his mind of his own complete fabrication) be best let rest for now. *They don't know that it's all been fucked from the start.* Commendable for seeking change, though. But it's all on rails. Inevitably oil will be out (in one way or another). It's still in its day, though. And it's had a hell of a run.

He'd often thought about building an electric vehicle. Maybe he would put an electric motor in this one. Though, this one was not a good candidate for an electric conversion. It was way too heavy to begin with, and it was about as aerodynamic as the broadside of a billboard.

He decided to glance at his phone. It had been long enough:

> *Francis*
> *Umm Hello ?*
> *Like are you gonig to*
> *come see me today or ..*
> *Ok Whatever*

Beatrice - Missed Call (4)

> *I cant fucking believe you*
> *Heelo???*
> *You obviously dont remember that*
> *you said you come over today*
> *You are so fuckign*
> *selfish fuck you*

It had been three days since Francis had seen Betty, his girlfriend of nearly two years. He could not recall his promise to meet with her that morning; not to say that a promise hadn't occurred, he just couldn't remember. He also wasn't so exactly sure Betty said everything she thought she did all the time. It all seemed so inconsequential to him. And although this barrage of language may be crass to some, that was the status quo with Francis. It wounded him every time. And though usually he said nothing, until, at times, he didn't.

Francis tried to recollect the certain something in his previous week with Betty and tried to dissect exactly what might have constituted a promise, or a supposed promise, to her. Perhaps a supposition or presumption was taken as a promise. It made really no difference to Betty. An acorn of an inclination was, to her, as mighty as a great oak itself. It really didn't matter, though. What mattered was that Francis was, at the moment, and whether by fault of his own or not, in hot shit.

The phone laid within view on the workbench where it had first been left first thing that morning. Francis thought of replying at that moment something quick and defensive; perhaps diplomatic. But to his better judgment, and simply because so much time had elapsed, a hasty reply was now moot. He read the messages again from the front screen of his phone; careful not to open the Messages app and unveil a read receipt. He had the time now to formulate a well crafted response, he figured. But he could not think of one. His mind was tired and he just didn't have it in him right now to go ten rounds. He read again, the expletives were three of a thousand cuts; tone and tact a deafening silence. He glanced among his things. His pursed lips and blank stare again fell heavily among the bric-a-brac.

Mopar Fest was coming up. Yes, it was coming up next month. That event was dutifully printed on the calendar that was hanging above the work bench. Francis couldn't help but fathom all those cars; all those enthusiasts. He couldn't help but think about the amount of money that would roll over those fields that weekend. He saw a classified ad in a magazine last year for the remnants of a '65 Belvedere; an original 440 car with an opening bid of eighty five thousand dollars. *Where do people get that kind of money,* he thought. *Is it mostly inheritors of old money? Was it the result of cutthroat capitalism? Either or,* he supposed; it didn't matter. Regardless, that's a lot of money for a hobby. *A hobby or an investment?* He didn't want to think about that but he supposed that's exactly the reason, or one of the main reasons, for the steady increase in prices of classic cars. There was almost no niche left untouched from the skyrocketing cost of these old things. You used to be able to get a deal on any old four door or straight six secretary-mobile, but not anymore. Francis was well aware that he had been the inheritor of wealth. He had inherited the Coronet in that very garage from his father, who bought it off Katherine, Beatrice's grandmother, who had possession of it when her husband passed away. They were all dead now, except Betty of course. This was certainly no eighty-five thousand dollar car though. But still Francis seriously contemplated what it was worth.

It seemed to Francis that they had all been alive not that long ago. Francis' dad well... he could still envision him hunched down beside that car doing spot welds on a quarter panel. He did most of the body work. It was very clear where his work ended and Francis' began and finished. But the metal was all in now. There wasn't any rot left.

He could see him hunched over the grille examining something in the engine bay; *God*, it seemed like it had just happened. That he had been there only yesterday and that he would be there again tomorrow.

He remembered the exhibition of yanking out the motor together and how nearly both of them met their demise in the act. But it got out; it got overhauled and it went back in again. That big dumb hunk of iron.

He reminisced about how he would work on one thing while his dad would work simultaneously on another. They weren't that close, though, he ruminated; not terribly. Those months they worked on that car had probably been the closest they'd been. It was a terribly clichéd scenario and Francis was aware and he hated it. But he couldn't have been more grateful it'd happened.

Francis thought bitterly about how his dad hadn't told him he had cancer until a week before he died. It was sudden and he didn't fight it. He had his reasons, whatever they may have been, which just left Francis alone in the garage; shuffling around thinking about it; staring at the Coronet; tinkering with his tools. Thinking about all the *why's* wrapped up in it. It didn't make sense to Francis and it was selfish if you asked him. Francis figured at the time he just thought age was catching up with the old man. He didn't notice any changes until it couldn't be denied any longer that something was up with him. He'd joke about him getting old and frail in their way and *God dammit* he felt like such an asshole now. Drake, the old man, told him eventually. He couldn't have known how much time he'd have left but it turned out it was almost none. Francis couldn't parse his thoughts on whether that was for the better or for the worse but settled for that was just how it was.

But Drake (no relation to the singer, he'd say), the old stubborn bastard, knew his time was ending. He could tell it was ending if Francis couldn't see it. He hated that singer and the fact they had the same name. Francis didn't mind him so much. He mostly just listened to whatever singles the radio played. Drake would say he was giving all the Drakes a bad name, naturally. *As if there were droves of drakes out there.* The man was insane the way he carried on sometimes.

They would talk about all sorts of things while they worked on that car. Drake, knowing all things, reckoning quietly at his being and dispersing automotive knowledge and the-like; and Francis, the knower of nothing; learning the subtleties of method and technique; they breathed life back into the machine. Drake would help as best he could with Francis' academics and general life advice. Francis would often just bounce ideas off Drake because he found he most often looked at things through a lens of pragmatism that Francis admired and was also most often unable to command. Though, most of his ideas and philosophies were so far out in left field they couldn't be repeated outside of the comfort of that garage. Francis learned a lot when it came to practical methods of things and tricks-of-the-trade. Lots of neat old mechanics tricks. Some methods were archaic (but also so entrenched within the old man that neither could do anything about them). One could only "uh-huh" and "mhmm" as he chugged along in his quarkie idiosyncrasies. He was a busy-body; a guys-guy who simply just *was*. How much did he move the needle in the Great Picture, who knows? A champion of attrition; not unlike most, was more like it. But a passer of knowledge; intangible, unquantifiable knowledge. A quiet story passing from one to another. Francis loved and loathed all of that about him.

"Some dents can be punched out from behind; like this..." he could see him again now, sitting half in the trunk, one arm acting the phantom holding a dolly from behind the sheet metal, popping out dents in the quarter panel with small strikes of a hammer from the other side. Others would need heat and some were where the body filler would do its thing. "This is where the serial number on the diff is. And these last three numbers here, you see? Those are the important ones. This one isn't special. Eight and a quarter; one wheel peeler."

"I wish I... you know... I wish I tried harder," he was sullen and deliberate. "You got to apply yourself at the right time. Right at the time when you're getting into booze and girls; it's the worst time, I know. Fifteen; around there. Guys I played with..." it was hockey, "I mean I played with them; on the same teams, you know? I could keep up with them. I remember this one year I was trying out for the rep team; this wasn't too far after we were into contact;

Atom I suppose; I was coming down the wing; left wing, ya; I played wing then before I switched to D; and this big fucker Kyle Brough; good guy; I remember looking for an option then glancing at the puck; the next thing I saw was the lights on the ceiling; he laid me out flat. I remember it didn't hurt though; I was fine. Him and I ended up being D partners a year later; or maybe that same year. He went on to play junior. Guys like that applied themselves at the right time. They took the next step, they got into junior or college, they stuck with it; they didn't dick around in highschool. Kyle didn't dick around; he didn't play any other sports even though we tried to get him to play them all; the guy was a beast; he was committed to hockey; he was playing junior and getting call-ups to the "O." Then, you know, some of them got into booze too hard or, well, a lot of them started stuffing stuff up their noses too... I mean, that happens; that's a big part of applying yourself and staying focused at the right time. I don't know. I've worked with guys that know guys in the Show and they've told me stories of their brothers being way better than them when they were younger, or his buddy was way stronger and way faster; better shot; some played in the "A" too. Now he's running equipment for his buddy's uncle. I should have just ran 5k a day, did some push-ups – crunchies...I should have..." "I don't know...looking back now...I don't know..."

At the time, Francis didn't know what he was aiming at; being twenty two at the time it was too late for him as well. What his dad told him wasn't advice (although, it perplexed him why he didn't tell him this when he was that age. Or maybe he did in a weird indirect way; the way teenagers are most of the time; only hearing white noise from their parents, he might have Francis couldn't know for sure). It was a weird repentance is what it was; that was all.

There was free advice on women too (of which, of course, he was a grand ol' artificer of love – being twice divorced): "They're all the same, son. Just pick one and ride it out 'til you die." "Mhmm." Francis had confided in him, much to his later regret, about a recent incident between him and Betty. At a wedding of a friend - a good friend, of which he was a groomsman, actually. Beatrice ended the evening by getting incognizantly intoxicated and had the police arrive at their hotel room door at two a.m. With Betty thoroughly unconscious, Francis remained in the threshold of the doorway stumbling through an explanation of how she couldn't tolerate alcohol with the medication she was on (a truth). However, the situation had reached its precipice only moments before screams of an insidious (and unintelligible) argument pounded through the hallways of that cheap hotel. To say the evening ended on a definite false note would be an understatement. But as the two burly policemen questioned; and a dull tom-tom began inside Francis' brain, he politely diffused their inquisition. Francis closed the door and slithered back into the bed with sleeping Judas.

Francis had beat her; which was news to him. And much to the shock of all; and there were many friends in rooms that lined the hallway of that hotel staying there as well; some heads poking into the hall and eyes peering out of doorways of dimly lit rooms. Eyes of friends; eyes he dare not meet in dreams. He tried to not think of them; there are no eyes here. Certainly not here beside the paralyzed force that lay beside him; a shade without colour. No one dared to intervene; no one could make sense of what was happening. But the embarrassment pulsed through Francis like steam in a pipe with no way out. Her brother was coming to kick his ass, she screamed at him. For what exactly, Francis wasn't sure; only moments ago the evening was going fine. Also, her brother; who wasn't much of an imposing force; would, if actually called, be more perplexed than anyone. But he would also be, more than likely, understanding of the situation, as he knew how Beatrice was and he knew Francis fairly well and the two of them generally got along well. He knew Francis was alright and would never do such a thing. But him being a two hour drive away at the time made the situation all the more absurd.

There was a switch within her. And it had all to do with *that God damned medication*. She would be fine and jovial; the life of the party one minute, and then the next a silent wave washed over her. As quiet and nearly undetectable as a wave slipping up a beach in the dark of night, but to a keen eye, or one that's seen it before and knows what one's looking at, could be perceived if watched carefully. A moment within her of quiet introspection, or maybe the complete loss of introspection was more like it; but a moment is all it took. Then it was like the eye of a shark rolling back white. No one could know for sure, not even Betty; for she certainly couldn't remember. But suddenly Ms. Hyde would careen into the room; barbarous and violent and send the pleasantness of the evening crashing down as subtle as a car drives through a glass wall. It wasn't entirely her fault. Although, Francis thought she should know better by now. It was an odd thing, but it was almost always a certainty when the alcohol and medication met on the same corner.

"You don't need to be a driver like your old-man y'know? You know what I mean... You don't need to go into a line of work like that...blue collar schlub work, I mean. Go back to university; get a degree. You can...that'll put you in that, y'know, like, on another plain; on another plateau. The longer you go in between highschool and university the less likely you are to go at all. Fuck, you're already twenty-two, you'd've be done by now."

"...I'm tryin'ta teach you to, I guess, from my mista... from where I wished ...fuck, whatever, do whatever you want. I guess I wished, if I'd have done it all again...that's what I would've done."

"Actually, you know what? Go up into town here," he'd ramble on. "Ya! Shit, they'll put you through school and pay you to do it. That's right." He was talking about the Service because there was a base not too far from the house. "You have a job right there and you'll have a degree. Or you can stay with them and make a career out of that. Pension! Benefits! I never had any of that. Retire at fifty five. Look at John up the street: retired. Look how young he is. I don't even think he is fifty five. Ya, that's what you should do. You should go talk to him, or you should just walk down there and talk to a recruitment officer. Just get some info at least."

Just drive down there; just talk to a man. It was easy; just sign a paper; just ship up to Alert; to the end of the fucking earth; to some God-forsaken frozen hellscape. Or to Saint-Gerome-du-some-fucking-bullshit for eleven months to learn French. Eleven months, fuck that. Francis had briefly looked into that already. And that after all that gracious training and, of course, signing a four year commitment, you'd be obliged to accept an all-expenses paid, perhaps one-way ticket, to, one can be sure, some armpit of the globe. And how exactly was he supposed to broach that to Ol' Drake, "Uh, hey guy, it's 2009... you know there's a war going on right?" Francis was nearly certain that thought hadn't actually registered with him. It was also difficult not to be entirely cynical of the entities that place the pawns in the perils of other people's problems. They cry havoc; Francis cried foul. And he wasn't the only one. The main thing it boiled down to was that it just didn't sound like a good place to work. Especially after you got out, from what he'd heard. He'd known a few guys that had been through it and come out; he worked with two guys. Shrapnel in the back of one of them. The doctors removed most of it but there was a piece they decided to leave in, as the piece was so close to his spine operating would be more dangerous than leaving it in. He remembered one day his friend was looking more troubled than usual; aside from his regular mess of anxieties; but that day there was something else. Francis asked him what's up. Well, the government had given that fellow a letter with a cheque that day for one hundred and sixty three dollars for that piece of shrapnel. He said they sent it every year. Francis agreed that seemed like straight fucking bullshit and asked what his friend could do about it. His friend said not too much. Now all he did was write "F.U.C.K. Y.O.U." on the cheque, spit on it and sent it back. That guy had lost a friend while he was there too. The other guy Francis knew was more or less fine; he was in the artillery.

"You don't have to swing a gun, you know? You can sign up to swing a wrench," remembering Drake again. *How romantic,* he thought. Francis didn't know a lot, but he figured he knew well enough that you swing whatever they God-damned tell you to swing. Whatever that aptitude test tells you what to swing. Romantic would be a pilot, he conceded. But a romantic pipe-dream is all that is and the odds of swinging a wrench or a gun was a near certainty. He wasn't ready for that. He didn't think he'd mind the work. In fact, he often thought he'd be fairly competent at it. It was the lifestyle. He had seen the kids come and go; the kids of military families. They'd come, they'd stay, they were mostly nice, and then they were gone. They don't even round out a school year. A blip on the collective memory if remembered at all. *"Hey, remember Brad?" "He was here for like grade six for most of the year."* Francis didn't want that. He didn't want to subject a family to that; his future family, he supposed. He wanted one eventually or he at least wanted the agency to have one. Moving around at the whims of orders was not the way he wanted to live.

Francis decided it was about time to go into the house and wash the antifreeze off as the stinging chemical was now making his skin sticky and as it dried made it feel like a ferocious frenzy of pins and needles. It was becoming unbearable. He left the garage and went in the back door of the house which entered straight into the small dining room. The inside of the house was cluttered which was augmented by its smallness. Whatever the opposite of minimalism was, that was it. The dining room ("dining room") was at the rear of the house which he entered from the driveway at the back corner of the house. He navigated around the dining table which was no longer able to entertain a single dinner plate and felt far too large for the ten by ten room in which it was in. It had strewn upon it masses of papers constituting bills, rather important legal papers that should've been attended to, weekly flyers interspersed throughout, an ordinary salt and pepper shaker and an empty ceramic serviette holder with a rooster on it poking out from underneath the great mess. He began to trudge upstairs uncaringly marking the wall with his grimy fingers as he turned on the light for the dimly lit stairs. He didn't care at all about the grime. It was merely a *chef's kiss* on the general disaster of the place. He figured anyway that no one would notice the small mark he made on the world. There was no hallway at the top of the narrow stairs but only the bathroom directly ahead; his bedroom to the left; and to the right was now Mary's: the recent benefactor of his dad's stuff; including the house; Drake's girlfriend of the last eight years. *Frig, had it been eight years already?* Francis thought. *That conniving bitch.* She was nice in a way; the way veneered wood is nice; but eight years? His room was terrible as he glanced into it. He wished he could be a minimalist and live with only three or five things in a room. Clean and sterile like an Ikea display.

Like a monk. He fantasized about that as he slipped into the shower thinking of home decor. He simply had too much love for *things*. He valued his possessions. He loathed himself for thinking that way, but he saw a utility in mostly everything. He shouldn't be a slave to material things, he knew. But he also knew as soon as he got rid of something there he would be at the store the next week in need of that very thing he had just thrown away. He supposed that was the mindset of a hoarder. Although, Francis believed he had a long way to go for that. Beatrice called him a hoarder and he resented that. He resented her for thinking of him in that way. She just didn't get it. Although, what did he have that could not be replaced, really, when it came down to it? Nothing, he supposed. But what a wasteful way to live life.

He needed a new start. It was growing awkward by the minute with only Mary and him in the house; though he rarely saw her; ships passing in the night (or mostly peering around corners to avoid the awkwardness of being in the same room). It was the principle of it; the absolute gall of it. He was hoping one day she would walk in and tell him that she was deciding to put the house up for sale, and that she would give him what he was due so that they could both have a fresh start at things. That was more than fair in Francis' eyes. What was unfair was how day by day went by and Mary just kept living; carrying on as if nothing had happened. As each day passed her intentions became clearer and clearer. And that boiled Francis' blood. He boiled in the shower, washing the sticky antifreeze off; water turning to steam as it hit him. She was going to take the house and leave Francis with nothing. He supposed he could talk to a lawyer but he didn't know where to start and he certainly didn't feel like he had the money for that. He supposed she knew he didn't have the money for that, which, to Francis, was a vile notion someone could be so sinister. He just wanted to forget about the whole thing. *Why couldn't it all just work out?* He really didn't want to have to deal with legal shit in court; seeing his dad's legacy placed upon some desk like a grand trinket and be examined in front of the world. It wouldn't amount up to enough to pay the band for the fanfare so why even bother? What was likely more true was the fact that Mary couldn't stand Beatrice. For a brief moment in time Francis felt that Mary was trying to protect him in some weird way. She didn't want Bea to ever get close to a sniff of anything that came from that house. It wasn't her place to determine that, Francis felt. She loathed Betty for her frequent outbursts; often untimely nitroglycerin-fuelled meltdowns and her general crassness. Mary was old-worldly; stiff-upper-lip-bite- your-tongue-and-act-properly-at-all-cost; but still be a feminist and pious all at once. She was an armchair Catholic; a sure-to-attend-Christmas-Mass- but-as-for-the-other-fifty-one-weeks-of-the-year... She wanted nothing more than for Francis to cut Beatrice loose. For more than one reason you could infer what Francis thought of that. It would be the good Christian thing to do, of course.

He needed a little apartment somewhere. A small windowless shit-hole on the fringe of civilization to toil in. He could leave now; or soon at least; pack what he needed and start again on the far side of the city; he didn't need a lot. Maybe in another small town outside the city; there were a bunch; they were all similar to Francis. He didn't exactly grow up around there so he didn't care where. Came from away, as the Newfoundlanders say. Maybe he should go to Newfoundland. Any city or town or village or hamlet, really. Some desolate, echoey hovel; with all the air and light and time and space within which to punch away on, what would be, a workhorse of a keyboard. The fantasy of it made his blood pressure come down. But the reality that he didn't have money for first and last month's rent didn't bring it down too far. He had the car. The Coronet was his for sure; Drake wanted him to have it and signed the registration over to him. He also had a truck; much newer than the car but certainly older than new, which was worth hardly anything. And he wouldn't have to reply to that phone that was down the stairs, out the door and in the garage on a workbench that was off to the side. *Sell the car,* he thought. *Get some money; make that happen; that's the plan.*

He chugged down the stairs and out the back door to the garage. He was on a mission when, upon barbarously crashing through the threshold of the garage man-door, saw his father there toiling away. Again; suddenly in vivid recall he was there. His phone; his mission; his reply now seemed a light year away. He didn't know if it was the way the car was and how he'd seen it before; how he'd seen it so many times before; always exactly there, while his dad and he breathed life back into it. It could have been the familiarity of it all or something he noticed in a lightning quick glance or what he'd eaten for breakfast that morning, he didn't know. When he walked into the garage he saw his father leaning over the fender with his head in the engine bay and spoke to him something he'd heard before in that frankness that often caught Francis off guard, "Keep pace with the world, and remember: every time you get ahead means that someone has fallen behind." Francis' double was there too. Laying prone half under the car as his dad leaned against the car and orated to him. It was one of the last times they spoke with any meaning. Or rather, Drake spoke and Francis 'ummhmm'ed and 'yepped,' in his usual way. The old man's physical decline was in full display by then. Francis told him daily to go to the hospital but the stubborn bastard never did. Not in any way that Francis wanted anyway; not in any way that was to his betterment. He had gone and saw who he needed to see and confirmed the suspicions of his death sentence; and returned without telling Francis in so many words. Francis knew, in time, without the words what was happening. The moment was only that, although to Francis, as he stood there and watched that scene play out like a movie, it was as long as one. And then it was gone and he was alone, paralyzed three feet past the threshold of the man-door, immersed in the golden illuminated particulate floating in the air. And as quickly as it appeared, in reality, the vision of his father returned to the ether of that golden atmosphere.

Though he might not have known it instantly, that day with those words, an amoeba that for most of his life embodied that man morphed into an enigma. Over a course of time after that Francis tried earnestly to recollect every possible odd utterance his father had ever murmured to him. Had the duplicity of this creature slipped him? For his entire life had he been too young and naive or outright self-absorbed to notice who he really was? Maybe there was no duplicity at all; maybe he was trying to look for something that was never there. Or maybe his father never really took his mask off with him. Maybe he was always playing the part with Francis. Was it famous last words taken all wrong? Or was it just a compilation of quips and phrases one gathers over a lifetime; not really paying any mind to anything; just reciting things he's heard. The same man once said, never hold in farts; they will travel to the brain; give you shitty thoughts. So indeed some level of diabolical duplicity was in question. Francis replayed any and all quasi-cryptic quips he could recall in his mind since he'd walked into the garage and saw himself there with the phantom of his father as he puttered around some more.

It was a gorgeous car. It was a deep forest green that atomized into a bewildering universe of sparkling metallic flake that glittered when you got right close to it but looked solidly dark, almost black depending on the lighting, if you were to stand back only a few feet. He brought it down off the jacks and then it sat there properly in the middle of the garage. It looked like it could have been in a magazine. It could have its photo taken anywhere it was so photogenic. Even in a dusty, unspectacular garage (although dusty, old, unspectacular garages are part of the allure to most car enthusiasts' for whatever reason). It didn't have one bad angle to it, thought Francis. Some models of some makes could make a person be put-off a bit, like catching an actress some time in an unflattering way. But he didn't think this car had a bad side. It was gorgeous down to every nut and bolt. He suddenly became fantastically aware of how lucky he was that this car was sitting in his garage, and how it came to be there. It was

Betty's grandparent's car originally. Well, it was mostly her grandfather's car; his wife didn't drive. He passed; she didn't drive; and having no use for it, sold it for a miserly sum to a young neighbourhood lad by the name of Drake Barnes. It was pure coincidence that his son would happen to date their granddaughter years later. Though the matter of having a mutual connection by way of this vehicle was an inconsequential talking point in their early dating. Francis thought it was pretty wild, but to Betty it was an uninteresting anecdote. To her, a car was a car as any other. He could hardly believe it; she knew it was just the result of living in a small town.

The phone beat like a berserk robotic heart inching slowly across the surface of the workbench from where Francis had left it. He walked over to it, touched the top of it and gazed upon the tiny little monolith but there were no new messages. It was the same as before. The buzzing was from notifications of an app and the only messages were the ones from earlier. He felt guilty for not responding to Betty diligently. The thing was, he hadn't had it in him. But now blearily, he texted:

Hi

He waited for the show of the ellipsis but it didn't come. He waited for a while and wondered what it was that had distracted Betty. She was usually pretty prompt, except for occasionally when Francis needed her urgently. Then her phone was suddenly and mysteriously in a box en route to Myanmar or at the bottom of the Marianas Trench or God knows where. He felt his guilt grow as the moments passed. *Did she fall back asleep? Was she in the shower now? Was she staring back at her side of this dark portal? Was she writhing in loathing? Was she collecting herself?* The latter seemed improbable.

I thought it was Sunday we
Were supposed to hang out?

He had written but not sent: *I can come over today in about an hour* when he saw the ellipsis finally display so he deleted what he wrote. They were supposed to go clothes shopping for work attire for Betty's new job she'd be starting the Monday after next. What Francis was supposed to contribute regarding women's fashion confounded him, but he was going for support he supposed; she needed a warm body with half a brain to bounce her own ideas off and deflect her self-deprecations; at least that much was obvious to him. He genuinely couldn't remember now when they were supposed to go; or even if they'd made plans at all. Francis figured Beatrice had a way of massaging supposed recollections to fit her will. That was a nice, or rather diplomatic, way of putting it, thought Francis.

Its fine

I don't need you to come
I just wont go

                              Sorry I forgot,
                        I'll come over in an hour

It was nearly noon.

                                            K?

Time passed.

                              Is that alright?

You dont need to come over
You obviously dont care at all
Its fine
Your obviously too busy
I just wont start this job
Ill just try and get a job
that doesnt need
nice clothes

Don't be facetious

I don't know what
that means

...

You need new
clothes for this job
And it's not a big
deal for me to come over at all
I just need an hour
to get over there

Its fine
Dont come over

Bea don't be that way

Francis tried to call her but she would not answer and that aggravated him. He would go over to her place despite her saying not to; he knew she wasn't sincere when she said so. They would go shopping that day. He didn't want to, but he figured the repercussions of not outweighed a few hours of monotonous lingering and lurking outside of change room curtains, offering obsequious compliments through gritted teeth, pursed lips

37

and feigned excitement. Sitting in "*the chair*." What a joyous time it would be. He had nothing to do that day but that.

He walked over to the driver door of the Coronet, opened the big swinging thing and sat down on the bench seat. It had been recently reupholstered by a guy-of-a-guy he knew from work. He did a great job but it was expensive. Francis wished that he'd done the work himself. It was expensive enough that the rear seat didn't get done at the same time. It remained in the fifty year old hardened pleather that now had about the same amount of comfort as sitting on a sidewalk. But Francis never sat back there so it didn't matter to him. He gave the white hurst shifter a wiggle to assure its neutrality then grabbed the keys that remained in the ignition, gave it a click and watched the gauges wake and then he turned the machine over. Without hesitation, the once silent, tranquil morning erupted into a cacophony of violent sound and fury. On colder days the three eighty three would crank defiantly, but being as it was a warm summer morning it erupted in a cloud of richly fuelled high idling. The garage filled quickly with nauseating gas. After a few minutes, the electric choke walked itself back to a chugging idle. The truly toxic fumes of a slightly rich-running cat-less American V8 were quickly making the garage unbearable. Francis left the car and garage on account of it as he let the car warm up some more but he was glad he did because he realized his wallet was on the counter in the kitchen. He went in and got it, grabbed a few other things and got ready to leave the house. He came back out and walked into the now completely uninhabitable garage. He should have parked with the tailpipes pointing out the door but he found it easier to work on when it faced outwards. That was a lie. He really just liked the look of it when it faced out the opening of the garage door. That's what you had to do if you owned an old muscle car; that's the way everyone parks their muscle cars; it's just cooler that way, that's all. He enjoyed looking at it through the window of the house when the garage door was open. He thought for a bit that he might like looking at it more than he liked driving it. It truly was a beautiful thing. It didn't matter where it was or what angle you caught it from. It was like looking at a tiger in the zoo as it strutted by you, staring back at you with blind eyes that blazed like meteors.

He was surprised she got a job. For more than a year now she hadn't been working and the mere mention of work sent her into a crumbled mess. He thought she'd be on pogie from here on out. She hadn't even applied to any jobs. It was Francis that polished her resume; wrote her cover letter and applied on her behalf online. She got a callback on one and lucked out. Francis was thrilled, of course. This meant less time spent in her basement-dungeon-fire-trap of a windowless shit-hole apartment (Francis' opinion), and less time spent in week-old sweatpants. He thought, and he knew it was an outrageous idea but, that's what people should do: be out and about in a society of other people; communing; living; prospering. It seemed like an idea akin to shit-flavoured ice cream to some people. But he could see the stress of returning to work was taking a growing toll on her. It could have been the fact that she had been out of the workforce for so long that, in her mind, people were no longer using computers and smartphones but telepathy and Federation credits to hover through the brave new world she found herself in. Or it could have been the fact that her previous job's management were such disgusting elitist dickholes that it scared her from any type of work anywhere, ever. He assured her that it would be fine and a bit of nervousness and anxiety would be normal; anyone starting a new job would have those feelings. But Francis could see the toll it was taking was growing beyond something that could be sucked up and reigned in with a stiff upper lip.

He would've loved to stay in his garage. The Sirens of leisurely puttering on a weekday morning called out to him. He could stay there forever. Forget about everything past what he could see from the fifteen by eighteen foot space; a place that was like his own little deserted island. Free from the outside world with the exception of his phone which connected him to the entire planet. Screw shit-flavoured ice cream; this was different. At least he'd be marginally productive even if the only benefactor was him. No one would stop by. No one would disrupt his peaceful meandering within. He was alone. He didn't want to leave, but he had to. He decided to send another text to Betty. He did again, and again received nothing in return. So, he took a deep breath and stepped quickly to the Coronet. The air was unbreathable so he had to go. He hopped in quickly and slammed the big steel door. He put the car in gear and slowly feathered out to the driveway, stopping to close the garage door with the remote he kept on the sun visor. The windows had been down the whole time the car had been idling which he regretted now. The exhaust remained in the car as he pulled away. Once the garage door had closed he looked quickly for a clear road then set off onto it. Once straight he jammed on it a bit; he was sure to the chagrin of his neighbours; to clear the exhaust fumes out of the car.

What was that girl doing right now, he wondered? *Zoned out, twisting a lilac stock between her fingers? Contemplating the perfect response? Serving tea to friends? Yeah, that,* he thought. *Or, more likely, rolled into a ball in the womb of a warm duvet; sweating out overused antipsychotics and mood stabilizers with a television blasting to anesthetized ears.* That was the state he often found her in after he'd get off work and go over to her place. That's what he suspected she was really up to right now. He didn't know what the root of it all was despite his efforts to figure out why. Some days that was just the way he found her: in a puddled mess of unwakeable narcosis. Some days she'd be baking in a frenzy; firing off trays and trays of gluten free muffins, or making a five course dinner. Some days the TV was on and that was all. She wasn't texting back so he was left with little recourse but to head there.

She was waning on him. As he drove past the single yellow blinking light of his little hamlet; a non-thought of a place where people cutting through only had to inconveniently slow down; he watched the dark conifers and healthy hardwoods that lined the street row on row pass in perfect precession as he slipped into languid thought. Or at least he tried. He tried to think about Betty but nothing came. The trees row on row that led down to the recruitment office. He saw a quick face going the other way in a passing automobile; it got smaller as he stared into his cracked side mirror. He fidgeted on the bench seat as he tried in vain to get comfortable; he simply just never could driving that car. It had always felt alien to him. The long wheelbase; the super loose steering with a wheel of a cruising yawl; the bench seat like the shitty basement couch in someone's grandparents house where the location of each and every spring and wire was no mystery; a seat where you slid to and fro in each turn like a teacup on a table in a ship in a maelstrom. There was nothing like that around today; nothing made like that; not in more than a few decades. Bucket seats; rack and pinion; McPherson struts were all standard now. The uneasy feelings of vulnerability slowly tinkered, tightened and ironed out through decades of engineering. It made you as comfortable operating a three thousand pound machine as you would a washing machine or making a coffee. This thing was something wild; a thing made by chain-smoking alcoholics that believed the onus of safety be on a level head and people should be free to do what they want; if they wanted to kill themselves then they should be free to do so. When it got going fast it entered into some strange Twilight Zone effect; it was as if the car was acting on its own; just past the edge; and you were there just behind the edge, and it was calling you forward.

Francis watched the trees slowly slip by as if he was watching a coast slip by from a passing steamboat on a calm and steady river of asphalt. He watched it all slip by; the trees and what lies beyond and it was like thinking about an enigma. There was something out there. There was before him this smiling, frowning, inviting, grand, mean, insipid, or savage, and always mute with an air of whispering, *we are alone – come*. And the air was thick with the company of distant nations as they called out to him; their kinsmen. The passing landscape was almost featureless, as if still in the making, with an aspect of monotonous grimness. Although his current situation was no different; but devoid and vapid - it terrified him to look out there. The woods that line the street were lovely dark and deep, and he longed to pierce past them and be among those distant nations and kinsmen. A membrane retained him there. The curb kept the car on the road; the trees held the sidewalk and curb at bay; the light submitted to darkness beyond it all. This great traveling force, so immense and impermeable, it seemed to Francis that he was the only one that could see it and feel it. But he felt at the same time inferior before its grandeur; un-belonging to the great society, but still a sense of feigned superiority that he was among a select few that could at least feel the immense and impermeable thing. Feel something; *anything*. Through the heat reflecting back from the rearview mirror a mouth lectured, *hypocrite.* Could it be pierced, that membrane? By the tip of a sword or a pen it could be pierced. It had been done so by so many before; by worthy and unworthy alike. He knew one day he would walk by the curbs and trees that hold the universe in place. And you would see him one morning in the park reading the comics and the sporting page. *If you weren't so lazy, my fellow*. And you may join him too, if you can walk past your shadow at morning striding to meet you; past the curbs and trees that hold the universe in place. *My brother, you should read more.*

The idea that he would like to go into that insipid wilderness clawed on the inside of his skull; it had for some time; like a deranged prisoner in his final days on death row it dominated his mind. He thought briefly that he could go there. In a literal sense, he could go up to the hunt camp, he supposed. His friends' family camp where, from the age of eighteen, had hunted deer every November with an eclectic crew of guys that would bluntly solve the world's problems around the large maple table that was the feature of the one room cabin. Maybe he could set off from there into the frontier and build something; some shack; get squatters rights and be all set. A naive notion; but amusing; something to occupy his mind as he drove. He'd felt the feeling of a Frontier once in his life. A feeling he was sure was now nearly extinct from the human experience. While being shown a property after a long atv ride the property owner, on the summit of a great lookout, said, "This is as far as we've ever gone. You can go further but there's nothing else past here; it's just miles and miles of bush." It was just a feeling. It was something that couldn't be replicated, imitated or replaced with anything else. It was just a feeling. As far as being alone in the wilderness he figured most people don't realize the effect of being totally alone; even while in a cabin. The idea seems nice; even romantic to those that haven't truly been there when the sun sets and darkness fills an unlit room. That's quite a feeling too. He had done that once at the cabin; been alone for a night. To say he was unprepared would be understating it. Most people would never meet the person they'd find in that room alone, he thought. It terrified him, but he was glad he'd experienced it.

The phone buzzed on the seat next to Francis.

He replied, but there was nothing after that.

He had enough saved up for first and last but that was about it; there wouldn't be a dollar left if he scraped just that together. He could get an apartment on the other side of town; some roach infested tomb to rot away in. She would likely show up at his work after a while, but he could get another job too. He'd ghost her; like really, really ghost her. In another neighbourhood; in another place; in a different barely-above-minimum wage job he could get somewhere. How long could he keep that up for? How long would he need to keep that up for? Until she got the picture, he supposed. He could, or would, or maybe should sell the Coronet and then be set for a while. That was an interesting idea. He had his truck. But it was always such a pain in the ass to sell stuff online. A dreadful queue of losers lining up spilling their guts and lamenting days of old to him rather than opening their wallets. *Come on in, sit on the chaise and pine over that one car you had that one time -* he'd heard it ad nauseam. But he couldn't blame them. He'd been one of those losers; or rather, was one of those losers from time to time still; but in a different way, he supposed. Nothing is free, but money's expensive; that he knew. He would have to rough it out to some degree; deal with at least some amount of tire kickers in order to sell it. *Oh*, he loathed the notion of it. The Coronet already drew in enough people volunteering to chit-chat and chomp Francis' ear off; it might as well have been a billboard the way it stuck out among the contemporaries. He had certainly been asked enough if it was for sale. He could probably put a *for sale* sign on it. *Ah*, but then Betty would likely see it and wonder. Better to do it quietly online. He was still driving slowly down his road. He liked it there, for now, among the trees. He felt a great nostalgic flicker as he saw something in a farm field and had a fleeting memory of driving shotgun in his dads '77 Sierra Classic, where they'd drive slowly from field to field on their way to the back bush to where his dad would fell trees for firewood. At the hedgerow between each field they'd roll through slowly, peeking through to hopefully stumble upon a small herd of deer. They would pass an marshy bog on their way that had an old late-sixties Volkswagen Beetle that'd broken down eons ago with nature springing up from it everywhere it could. And he recalled the very real fable his older brother had told him that there were hundreds of snakes in that broken down car and that he can never get too close. He thought about his apartment and how he would have a milk crate for a chair and one plate and one fork and a few books and one slow laptop, or better yet an old mechanical typewriter, to do his work, drink coffee by the gallon, maybe start hacking darts by the carton and he would be happy. He would be content with that, he thought. He felt fine about selling the Coronet. The Coronet and a typewriter, he mused; as impractical and cliché as a typewriter was, to him they shared a sort of kinship. That mechanical self-reliance that made them completely autonomous. Feed one gas and oil and the other ribbons and paper and second-hand smoke; that's all they relied on. He liked them; he didn't care if they were cliché. He liked what he liked; both of those things.

When he would go back into the office of his work in two days to get his orders in the morning, he would have to explain to everyone over and over how he was doing. He wished he could just do one big speech to everyone at once and that would be the end of it. Or send out a memo to everyone to not mention anything. But soon enough, it would be over and the monotony of regular business would return and he would be left again to examine his life. Everyone already knew. He just had to sit through the condolences. He had to do it. He had to sit through it all. He'd try his best to get his orders in the morning quickly and race out to his service van and it'd be old news by lunch. Lives would trudge on and the years would pass as granules of sand slip through a fist holding sand. At least he had sand, he supposed. His apartment, fully formulated in his mind, glowed like a beacon now; it sang to him; it was a near certainty now. He buckled his seatbelt; that old dodgy lap belt that strapped him to his vessel so he couldn't jump out of his moving car and run straight at the first "For Rent" sign he'd see. He looked at his phone and Beatrice had not responded and in that moment it dug at him. Nothing is more painful to the human mind, than the dead calmness of inaction and certainty which follows, and deprives the soul of both hope and fear. He really wished she'd just text him back.

In a minute he would make a turn and continue on. He checked for his wallet again; and his phone; *yes, it was there on the seat,* of course; an automatic compulsion. It was always terrible to forget something. Get so far away from the house and realize your phone or your wallet is on the counter. Too far to go back now anyway; he'd just have to live without it if he had. He had everything; he knew that before he left. In a minute he would drive over a bridge and would undeniably no longer be in his familiar country.

The bridge intrinsically separated the quaint clusters of hamlets, small towns and villages that peppered the region to the caged, labyrinthian suburbs and ultimately to the dull grey downtown city proper, where the particulated ashy air of diesel exhaust battled the urine scented slime of the sidewalks for the title of most undesirable quality; that's what came to Francis' mind when he thought about down there anyway. That was mostly downtown, but Beatrice didn't live far from there. She lived on the north west side of Chinatown where it abuts Little Italy to the south but her sidewalks weren't much better. Francis didn't like it. He could smell the smell now and he loathed so much of it from the driver's seat of the Coronet doing about ninety at the moment. Just over the bridge, now coming into view, was the catacombs of the ever expanding suburbs and they were so much worse.

From the decay of downtown oozed an ever expanding lifelessness. It seemed to Francis that it spread outward like a wound trying to heal but only festering without the patient knowing it. It felt more like a rat maze than the eminence of a rat race. It was all a despised whirling maelstrom; a cacophony of horridness at which the center lived his love. That's where his work was too. Everything seemed to be there. He had to go there. And the bridge was out; under construction, anyway. *For frig's sake,* thought Francis. A flagman greeted Francis with a stop sign at the approachment of the bridge. The Coronet's radio played quietly above the chug of the motor; peppered by a bit of static. He could see the boys had done a number on the asphalt. It was completely torn up. There were piles of aggregate here and there and other supplies and machinery everywhere. This bridge was getting the full treatment. The flagman; oh, this great old grubber, with his wild white hair, wielding his pole which permitted or denied the passage across the river, was settling in for what he knew was to be a long while; leaned on his leaning spot. So, Francis too reclined the bench seat slightly and slid marginally down the smooth, but sticky from the heat and sweat, pleather seat. There was no way around, Francis knew, but a grand detour down along the river to the next bridge and then to double back again. It would be faster to wait even if it was for a little while. The petty pace of men and machinery trudged amid the bridge. Francis reached to turn the volume up on the radio. It was not the original radio but it was nearly of the era. It had the luxury of FM and Francis tried to recall if FM was an option in 1970. *It was an option*, he thought. *Rare though*, he believed. *Or, wait, was it available in '70? 71*. He had it dialed into the classic rock station. That station had the strongest signal and was really the only radio station that came in clearly for him. Styx was playing. He thought about turning it down again or trying to find another station but his indifference took the day and he left it alone and rested, watching the flagman between increasingly long blinks. A wild looking, grizzled old man with white hair and a forty year beard. For a moment it looked as though the man had seen all there was, is, and all there ever will be. And, as he looked curmudgeonly at the ground, Francis wondered how much of the world he'd actually seen. Nothing but the steady drum of traffic and the commanded flash of the *stop* and *slow* of his sign. His staring at the ground was suddenly interrupted and his eyes shot like a rifle shot to Francis as a loud wailing pounded within the Coronet. Francis sat up, concerned as he analyzed what was occurring with the car. It was turning its teeth against itself. Alternator seizing? The voltmeter was surgically steady. *Is a pulley loose? Water pump? Jesus, what is this? What is happening? A rod going? A valve let loose? Top end? What?* In a few agonizing moments the pounding lessened and became less frequent and a few moments later it ceased entirely; the car settling back into its normal rhythm. That was strange and concerning to Francis. The eyes of the flagman returned to his business on the ground. Francis could see on the other side of the bridge over the short pines that lined the edge of the river, church steeples of what he thought was a Catholic Church and another of a United one. The old grey stone was dwarfed by the giant white arches of the bridge. He wondered how much longer he'd have to wait. He should have been getting out and checking under the hood as to what that sound was. But he just sat there. He grabbed his hat from his head and checked inside before placing it back upon his head. Something was taking a long time; an unusually long time. There was no traffic coming the other way on the bridge and there hadn't been since he got there. The absolute detritus of the surface of the old bridge barred the lane in front of him. The muddy sluice from the work was running down from the bridge and underneath the area in which Francis had been ordered to stop. Francis watched the flagman grab his radio that was affixed to his mostly unbuttoned shirt. He was listening, not talking. The next thing he observed was him walk about fifteen feet to the bridge's edge, grab a wooden barricade which he then laboured back and placed it near his original position. Finally, in dramatic malaise, an arm swung like a pendulum with a gesture from the other, he signaled to turn right and take the road down the river to the next bridge. There was no crossing here now. And suddenly the iron rebar which stuck out of the bridge deck became a solidified rampart. Leave this place; he was not welcome here.

The river was as still as the landscape surrounding it as he drove alongside it. It was about a hundred-fifty meters across, he figured. *Tough go to swim that*, he thought; *with the current and everything* (he wasn't a strong swimmer). He thought about that part in that book, the *Bell Jar*, which he had recently read, about where 'Esther' tries to swim out to that island about a mile out, only to get intentionally tired and drown herself. Only that she couldn't and kept popping up like a cork. He didn't think he could make it across that river if he tried earnestly. He had a memory of his swimming lessons when he was a young kid. They used to give out little badges for each swim level you passed. He remembered that he couldn't float. He'd tried in vain and simply could not. Bones of stone, he guessed. He still can't float. He never got his badge and he remembered his mother asking him that day at the public pool; the day he failed; if he really wanted to do this and he said, no he didn't. He could hold his own in the water now, he supposed. And now and again he would try, in spite of God and dense blood and bones, to float. In a pool; in a lake; in the salt of the ocean. But he couldn't pop up like a cork no matter how hard he tried. He feared death by water greatly.

Francis kept driving down along the riverside. It was a pleasant drive along the water after the stone and dirt of the construction site had flung off the tires. The water was sparkling around the bend and it was clear if one could overlook the empty bottles, sandwich papers, silk handkerchiefs, cardboard boxes, cigarette ends and other testimonies of summer inculpations. The road twisted as the river twisted. The river sweats oil and tar, but it looked nice from afar. It's hard to say when it was most beautiful. Water in which you're most familiar is just that. So familiar you're aware of all its skeletons. This river was fine, it was just Francis' opinion on it. But sure as a one-legged tin-man shits in the woods he wouldn't be caught dead swimming in it.

The road flowed in lockstep with the river as it serpentined alongside a century-old stone retaining wall about three to five feet high depending on the height of the grassy bank to which it held back. The wall was right at the edge of the road and felt very close while driving in the seven foot wide land yacht that was skirting alongside it. The bank was, in most places, about a thirty yard climb up a steep grade which met a guardrail above; or a hedgerow; or the back of a fence to the houses that were up in the neighbourhood overlooking the river. The embankment was sparsely peppered throughout with trees that were mostly pine but the odd maple sapling gripped the bank for dear life. A small elm or beechwood would sometimes stand alone. Only the hips and gables of the houses could be seen from below when they could be seen at all. The bank would now and again dip down and a snapshot of a neighbourhood would be revealed for a moment. It was a beautiful neighbourhood along the river. Old stately houses built when the city was young gripped the prestige of the waterfront with cold stagnant hands. The road would go on for a bit up near the university, under an overpass, do a full loop and come to the road that had been just traveled under. Francis saw a few drops of rain appear on the windshield and didn't love the idea of being caught out in the rain with the Coronet so decided to pull over on the dirt shoulder beneath the underpass when he got there to see if the rain came. He would at least roll up the windows in case. The sun at that moment had been dulled by a dark cloud that looked like it had the potential to pour so he waited for a minute. It was otherwise still a beautiful day. The sun was seemingly still shining everywhere else except where he was. The office buildings to the west of him in the downtown core were now visible and still shining in sunlight. The dirt on the shoulder of the road under the bridge was dry like powdered dust. The slanted concrete leading up to the bridge deck was dusted in a fine powder as well and as his eyes climbed up the slabs of concrete they became fixed upon a mural on the wall just under the bridgedeck. Francis couldn't believe his eyes weren't drawn to it immediately. In awe-striking detail spread against a concrete canvas lay an intricate and masterful mural. It had the violence and dizzying busyness of a baroque hellscape and was deserving of a spot in any museum. There had to be dozens, if not hundreds, of gnashing and flailing shades, some on burning mountainous rock with others lashing in a lake of fire and all consumed in the red atmosphere and horror of it all. It must have taken months to complete. Francis was completely gobsmacked; he couldn't believe that this was here. The sky was still darkening over the bridge and with all but the driver's window now rolled up he sat in his seat frozen in utter awe. This must have been fairly recent work. It was mostly covering all the other murals. Those being the big words that graffiti artists love to do; or at least seemingly loved to do in the nineties anyway. Francis thought it completely justified and proper for this work to take precedence over those others; though he admittedly didn't know much about graffiti etiquette he could objectively say that this was more worthy. Someone, if it was the artist it couldn't've been known for sure, though Francis suspected somehow that it was the artist, had written in semi-hurried font "No Way out 'Dis City." That must have been the artist, Francis thought. He wondered who could have done such an impossible thing. It was perfect. It was perfect as he ogled it while he rolled the windows up in his car and then afterward just sat there staring out the windows. It was perfect until Francis' eyes landed upon the most grotesque part of the whole painting; that painting of hell. Someone; some asshole, had tagged, in that shitty little way that idiotic-pieces-of-shit tag things, the upper corner of the mural. Right there; some scribble. It was, to Francis, the most awful and disrespectful thing a person could do. Customs or etiquette be damned, this was something different. In the lower corner there was another. Francis was enraged. The callousness; the insidiousness; the absolute gaucheness because of the will of some empty headed ding-dong. He felt as if the work was his own, he couldn't imagine how the artist would feel. It was akin to someone scribbling with a sharpie on the Birth of Venus or the Son of Man. It was a perfect thing - and then it wasn't. The sky above the bridge brightened as if a Holy spotlight had been turned on and the threat of rain was gone in an instant and the heat returned.

Francis was still pissed as he drove on around the circle of the ramp that went up and merged onto the traversing four lane street on top of the bridge. He was halted at the end of the loop where the road merged by the volume of traffic. He waited as a nauseating procession of tightly bundled cars crept by. There was no way to merge so he waited. If he looked to the right he could see the large buildings, the same ones he'd seen along the river, being scorched in the sunlight. He was in the city now. He would have to wait for someone to let him in so he sat there patiently, craning his neck. In some ways he liked Downtown. Now and again there was an old stone heritage building peppered in among the new stuff; ghosts of an old town standing quietly in a wild whirlwind. He wasn't too far from the Peace Tower; he liked it down there; the buildings at least. The old stone, oxidized copper-roofed Gothic revival style buildings and large manicured lawns contrasted the pale monoliths across the street. All of them were burning sepulchers of any and all things Good in the world. They were neat buildings though, he might drive by there if he got a chance to.

Some nice soul begrudgingly let Francis's slow relic of a vehicle finally merge and he proceeded down the street in the shadow of the large high rises past the shaded shops that lined the ground level of the tall office buildings. The street and sidewalks here were calm the way a whacked beehive is calm. People came and went in total bedlam: in and out of shops and offices; crossing the street, darting between parked cars, buses and street vendors. Cabs, cyclists and pedestrians danced among one another in an undirected, intoxicating ballet. Through the chaos Francis would frequently find himself getting on the Coronet more than he'd like in order to survive the onslaught of traffic lights, merge lanes and stampeding hordes of traffic of both foot and auto. In more than one instance when he would get on it, Francis would observe a neatly oiled beard snap around the shoulder of a plaid shirt. Angelheaded hipsters with eyes fixed upon their hands circled the city blocks. There were many of them. The plaid shirt, in nearly every instance, would keep walking and the beard, spun round, would often scoff or grimace under its steady self-affirmation. On multiple occasions Francis witnessed a near collision to something within that busy beehive as a result of a forward moving body and backward looking beard. He thought, I have seen the best minds of my generation destroyed by indolence; half cooked notions and too little knowledge regarding too many things. Starving; hysterical; naked, mindlessly walking in their purposeless circles at dawn looking for their angry fix. Empty headed hipsters burning for their heavenly connection directed by the superstar dynamo in their podcasts. Shirtsleeves caught in the machines that molded them and unaware of their predicament. Empty-headed might be an understatement. Though, he couldn't truly tell who was wrong. He knew they weren't entirely wrong to scowl. But for certain their opinions differed. Francis knew he was caught up in his own ideas. Likely wrong on most, but he'd never admit it if it were true; and he wasn't hurting anybody, he figured. There was a palpable and visceral disdain emanating from some individuals directed towards him and the Coronet. They might have ideas of ride sharing and new electric cars as the bright and shining future. Francis had no qualms with either of those things but he did have his reservations about something new versus something fixed. The life of everything is a set timepiece once spun. It's up to everyone to spin it again. Everything isn't meant long for this world; and he knew it was everything, to be true. He knew the big tides of change (driven mostly by those fashionable plaid shirts) wouldn't be soon, but it would be inevitable. He also believed it would be less homogeneous than people might want or expect. He knew the human mind liked easy-wholesale answers to complex problems but he knew the future was hybrid (not in that kind of way). So he drove his Coronet. The ebbs and flows of all popular machinations will be fads in time; ideas too, even. *Yeah, yeah*, he thought. *There's more than one way to save a cat.* Francis valued his agency now, and always, but he also liked the prospect of the future. He loved the brave new horizons that were dawning and knew they would only get better. He wasn't a Luddite, but he appreciated *if it ain't broke don't fix it;* or better yet if it is broke, fix it. Why shouldn't he trust new ideas? Everyone trusted the gas engine for a long time. It was still a reliable thing if you could feed it. That confounded infernal inferno machine; eating the earth on which it did its work. *A perfected, flawed thing.* Those angel-headed hipsters will be sinning fathers too, in time. Everything needs to be fed.

He had heard the voices, he had heard them all. At the cocktail parties; everything was wrong with everything else. Rideshare... Hyperlinks... chainlinks... *"Change."* Change is inevitable; resistance is futile. He had heard conversations that people will never give up their right to drive their own automobile. They'd never trust a robot with their life. Much like everything else, the future is symbiotic; synergetic; but mostly organic. It's all organic; always has been.

He could feel the jeers of those backward walking heads from each block as he traveled down. He also saw the smiles and up-turned thumbs too, as if from Caesar himself. Attention, good or bad, is what he got wherever he took that car anywhere. Francis liked only the machine. The majority of people, he supposed, were completely indifferent. It was a car like any other; just like how Betty thought of it. There were lots of people walking along the sidewalks out on break, meeting with friends, grabbing something to eat or running some errands. It seemed like an endless flow of people trudging around and around the city blocks. Unintelligible in the flash of a moment. The way that a crosscut of a beehive looks in a quick glance: only bees coming and going in the line dance of their ways. One can't tell what any particular one is doing at a quick look. The yield hidden in the dizzying madness of it all. Each with their shoulder to the wheel; drudging the colossal Thing forward. It was a horrific sight. And in a few days Francis would be back there among them. The women in business-wear; the lamenting garbage men contemplating life and jazz; the innumerable noose-tight neckties and dirtied shirtsleeves of old men. The grey buildings fused into the like-colour of the sidewalk and that of the road which was drawn over like a pale white hospital sheet by the still and silent sky. It was a great opaque homogeneity, broken only by the people that crossed in front of it as they paced around the city blocks. Francis got another thumbs up amid the stern and solemn faces. He had not thought life had undone so many.

He drove on; caught up in the stopping and going of the great urban ebbs. It was rough going; mind numbing and a true test to not have one lose one's shit; but this was the next best way to get to where Beatrice lived since the bridge that would have been the easiest way was impassable. The Coronet was running ok despite the petty pace of traffic; that weird noise from earlier had not returned since. The temperature gauge was just above average which wasn't so bad considering the heavy traffic. All in all, the Coronet was a massively out place thing to be there among all those efficient machines on a weekday morning. Driving among the grey monolithic catacombs of the downtown streets and the bleak dust which drifts endlessly through its halls, one perceived, in a flash, the empty eyes of a Hakim Optical business. Within its gigantic and obnoxiously neon orange frames – there were no retinas. There is no face but only an empty persistent stare into eternal blindness. It was a nation-wide spectacles chain. There were locations in every decent-sized town across the country and many more in every large city. The empty eye-less orange frames Francis passed were dull with apathetic attendance and then were gone. Left alone to gaze emptily upon the hipsters and business men and women and bureaucrats and everyone else that passed by that often empty business. There was no one watching from those soulless frames. Francis drove by that place; the inactivity inside mirroring the inactivity out.

He came upon his sign for an apartment for rent. It was on a small door that he could see which led directly to a stairwell that went up to the apartments on the second level above a sushi restaurant. Above the eatery there was a small bay window protruding out from the building and next to it was a little iron balcony (or, rather, a fire escape with a little chair and table on it). Francis thought that would be a nice place to live. You could hang out in that bay window and see up and down the street. *How neat that must look at night. Yeah, that'd be great,* he thought. *You could sit and have a couple drinks on a small table on that little fire escape landing. That'd be pretty sick on a hot summer evening. Probably get pestered every couple of months by the landlord for having shit on the fire escape.* He'd keep putting it back out there if he did. This street wasn't busy with people in the evening when all the government workers that were here during the day returned to their homes in the suburbs. The downtown was virtually deserted after five o'clock. And the drastic contrast created an eerie feeling. The times Francis had been kicking around downtown in the evening or night time, going to or from friends' apartments or to bars or restaurants or wherever, it felt like a zombie apocalypse movie; it was so dead. In a few long blocks Francis would turn onto another similarly sized street, head up a bit through Little Italy and be in Beatrice's neighbourhood at the north end of it.

Francis glanced at his phone that he had pinched under his thigh on the seat. A solitary text message was there from Betty. It read:

It;s funny how you
just don't get it

At a light Francis sneaked a replied:

What?
What isit that
I don't get?

Francis was slowly approaching the corner to which he would need to make his turn. There were two cars

in front of him not turning. He knew he shouldn't needle
her into an argument while he was driving but he couldn't
take it back now.

I need to do dishes

OK

Ok

Francis watched the ellipsis appear and then vanish.

I can't

Why can't you?

Nevermind

*I'll help yo with
them when I get there.*

Whatever

what

Its fine nevermind
dont worry about it

Holy fuck, thought Francis.

I thought you weren't coming
over anyway

I don't think at any point did I insinuate that I wasn't coming over, he thought to himself.

No I'm coming over like I said
I'm on my way

He wanted desperately to be at home; alone in the garage; tinkering away; sorting nuts and bolts and puttering around. It was getting hot in the car as the mid morning sun rose. He was thankful for the shade of the tall buildings but he would've liked to get moving on and get some wind going through the car. His mind was wandering to this and that as he plugged along when heard a sound that made him rigid like the sudden sight of a snake might make almost anyone rigid. *Fuck*, he thought. A sound that came from outside the car that could be heard over the sound of his own engine and slicing above the moderate drone of traffic. He knew instantly what the sound was. He heard the sound well before he saw what, or rather who, it was. The sound was an obnoxious (understatement) of a muffler the size of a trash can that was attached to the underside of early thousands Honda Civic (*"Si"*). Robert James Martel: Mental; Bobbi Jones; BoJo; pick one. Francis could think of a few other choice ones as well. Again, he heard the obnoxious rip of Bobbi's aftermarket exhaust sound out from a heavy downshift shortly before he saw his car pull up to the lights to the left of the intersection Francis was stuck at. He was on the cross street and was going straight up the road that Francis would be eventually turning right on. The man (overstatement) had taken his economy car with the muffler and the "weight reduced" stripped shell of an interior; all the dents; scratches; cold air intake; painted valve cover; spray painted hood; requisite low profile tires and everything and everything and managed to create something that, if described as a colossal piece of shit, would be a bombastic compliment. Bobbi Martel was a different level of annoyance. Now Francis really wished he was back in his garage. Though, he was left with little options than to creep slowly towards the intersection

Well if you actually
were coming
over you'd be here by now

What the fuck? thought Francis, *She should know how long it takes to drive to her house.*

Francis watched as Bobbi's light turned green and he went straight through the intersection. He just didn't get it. So much time and money put into that piece of shit. Any of those four-banger economy cars; guys thought they were the fastest shit-on-earth but the truth was not that they had fast cars but that they all just drove like complete assholes. Bobbi was no exception; perhaps, the biggest asshole of them all. An irrationally weird kind of delusional. He'd take on the MaLaren Team if given a chance and believe he could win. *Believe.* He had more skull than brains. The Civic took off from the light with another typical obnoxious rip and then suddenly let off and slowed down briefly before jamming on it again and Francis knew he had been seen.

Bobbi had always wanted to race Francis in his Coronet. The two young men worked together. Every day after work when everyone was standing around waiting to go home Bobbi would ask Francis when he was bringing in the Coronet. He might have been slightly incredulous that he had a 1970 Dodge Coronet, despite the photographic proof. It was never road worthy enough to rely on to get into work and Francis really didn't want the smoke if he brought it to work even if he could. They could shut down the road the shop was on and do it right, Bobbi'd say. A threat Francis believed was possible as where their work was wasn't on a busy road to begin with. The other guys at work would love to see how that would go down and would certainly block an intersection or two to see it happen. Any given nice Friday at quitting time in the summer more than a few of the guys would light up the tires of their pickups or wives Subaru's or whatever they were commuting. Francis absolutely loathed the idea of racing on a public road, especially within the city. Not that he raced at all in any case but it was the idea of it to him. Maybe he was just too much of a straight-edge. At any rate, he'd much prefer to go to a proper drag strip, though he had never been to one. Or at least a straight country road. There were plenty of near perfect county road drag strips that were just outside the City. He didn't like that idea any better; he didn't want to race the Coronet, period. Still, a proper drag strip would be better than a pot-holed excuse for a road in the city where anyone could dart out in front of you or any number of other things could happen. *Fuck, what if you killed someone?* You'd do a bit of time over a dick measuring contest with *Bobbi Mantel. Fuck that guy.*

Francis thought about going straight to avoid him for sure. But if he did he wouldn't be able to turn right again for a while for the road merged shortly thereafter with another main artery and he'd be forced down a long way and he wasn't quite sure how he'd get back in a reasonable way. He could go straight and just pull over for a bit and do a u-turn before he hit the merge and turn back again on his intended route. But he didn't like that idea either. And after a few more minutes of stop-a-go lurching he decided enough time had gone by and Bobbi was likely long gone by now. At least he didn't hear that obnoxious exhaust anymore. He stayed in his lane which had the option to go straight or to turn right. He couldn't see down the cross street because of the building which presently obstructed his view. The apartment building, *or, office building? Apartment building*. It had concrete stairs that stretched the length of the building down about ten or twelve steps to a kind of – well Francis didn't really know what to call it. Kind of a plaza; not quite an arcade; below-grade-terrace kind-of-thing but the building itself, supported by its columns, was the roof over half of the space. It was essentially a below-grade open-air space you could cut through if you were walking around and were up for dealing with the stairs. It could have been a nice spot for a café and it looked like that's originally what its intention was. But all it was was a barren, tan coloured wind trap that swirled dust around in miniature tornados. It was a bowl made of concrete and you had to look down the stairs to see a little glimpse of the shop signs that gave the place a little splash of colour but was otherwise entirely bleak and void. Topping the stairs there were concrete flower boxes that wrapped around the block on the boulevard which were also void of life; full of stagnant dried dirt and cigarette butts. Francis had loitered around those planters before. Waiting for friends to buy smokes or chips in the depanneur below. He tried to look under and through that space down the streets but he couldn't and he had to wait until he inched past the corner of the building until he eventually could. He didn't see Bobbi and his Civic.

So, Francis turned the corner. The traffic on this street was lighter but still slow. It was a bit of a jog up to Betty's place from there yet. Betty's apartment was a crude

67

ad-hoc illegal thing that a friend of a friend of a friend of the family had set up in their basement. She moved in there after she left university. She didn't want to give the impression that she had failed at school and needed to move back in with her parents so she just needed a little time and space to recuperate temporarily until she figured out what it was exactly that she was to do. Or at least that's what Francis figured. She wasn't going back. The new semester had already begun.

Francis tried to consider how many kilometers he was from her house. He ruminated a bit on that and then decided it was a bit silly to try and figure out kilometers in the city. *Probably about four or five kilometers,* he thought. *As the crow flies. Thirty? Fifty blocks?* It was hard to say. The highway was probably about half way and that was at least a dozen blocks away for sure. Then down through Chinatown to the east side of Little Italy. It would be about twenty or thirty minutes, he supposed. *Jesus,* Francis had a minor panic attack as he looked down to see his fuel gauge needle touching the *'E.'* He thought he had over a half when he left but he must have been wrong. Sometimes those old fuel gauges were a little wonky. He had a ninety-one Silverado that was terrible for that; he loved that truck; he shouldn't have got rid of it. He knew there was a gas station right there up on the left once he turned the corner. He would have to cross two lanes of traffic though. That gas station was alright; he had been at that one quite a few times. The gas stations downtown were all pretty tight to get into; every one was always busy. Not exactly ideal to try and dock a land-yacht in but, hopefully, if this one was relatively quiet it wouldn't be so bad. Francis was chugging along slowly in the moderate traffic. There seemed to be something hindering progress every ten feet or so. Scarcely would a flow of traffic get up to anything amounting to consistent travel. There were taxi's merging in that particular way that they merge, motorists giving berth to cyclists, people braking for reasons unbeknownst to...reversing in the *middle of the lane, Jesus Christ! What is this Dingdong doing,* thought Francis. He tried his best to remain calm in the chaos of some people's idea of ordinary life. *What the fuck is wrong with people?* Francis then heard a sound that was as familiar as an old friend's voice and as detestable as a rat dragging its slimy belly on a riverbank. His stomach sank as he heard the rip of a four cylinder motor into a three dollar muffler. He could hear him but he couldn't see him. But Francis knew that he had been seen again.

The traffic slipped away ahead of him as he stopped and waited for an opening to turn left into the gas station. The front end of the Coronet creaked as it bucked over the raised sidewalk. Francis pulled in beside one of the open pumps. It was tight but fine; it wasn't that busy there but still, as with mostly everywhere he took that car, he could feel instantly all eyes dart towards the Coronet. All he hoped was that he could buy his gas in peace and not answer a million questions from some stranger in dreadful chit-chat, or listen to the lore of days-of-olde as some old fucker pined about the car he once had forty years ago. Francis simply could not give less of a fuck. He shut the car off, got out and did his thing at the machine. The cost of gas was, as always, outrageous. He didn't have the money to fill it up so he put in what he figured would get him to about half. Francis scanned the lot. There was a guy in a black Hemi Ram subtly taking particular interest in the Coronet. There was an older woman in a Tuscon that had pulled in after Francis that was squinting at the prompts on the pump. The traffic on the street seemed to be moving briskly. By the road there were two sapling maple trees that had been planted when the gas station had been renovated with two small birds chasing one another from one tree to the other. Francis looked inside the store and murmured aloud, *Oh shit*, inside he saw his friend Youssin. He had forgotten that he had a job there. Truth be told, he couldn't keep straight the amount of jobs that Youssin had got and lost or left; sometimes within the same weekend. It was a point of comedy how frequently he got fired or quit. About two weeks, he'd say, was his average for holding down a job. Sometimes he'd leave; from boredom or something better would come along; sometimes they'd tell him they didn't see a future there for him. Francis knew one time he got fired from a night shift at a fast food place because he just crushed book after book instead of doing anything. He read a lot. He suspected that was the case for most of the firings a lot of the time. Never anything crazy He was in university and it was only part-time jobs. It was always something like working fast food or at a gas station or in a warehouse or something. Francis wouldn't say the two of them were close, but they ran in the same circle and had been to most of the same parties over the last year and a bit. Acquainted enough to go in and say hey at least. He was a good lad; always happy; always the biggest shit-eating smile on his face. Almost suspect it was so big. As if he was fresh off of eating an entire tray of weed brownies. But it was so prominent and unflinching that it must have been genuine (although, yes, he was probably pretty high a lot of the time too). He seemed like a genuine guy, anyway. Francis walked across the lot and into the glass fronted building. The Coronet remained in the shade of the gas pump veranda; tinging and hissing from the hot contracting metal. Through the storefront glass Francis and Youssin conversed. The birds in the maples tussled once more and flew off; two cars honked impatiently at a third not moving at a green light at the intersection nearby; the guy from the Ram walked over to check out the interior of the Coronet as it tinged and pinged. It wasn't for about ten minutes until Francis and Youssin said they'd see each other later and Francis exited the glass box and walked back to the Coronet. About half way back to the car he stopped and noticed something on the ground. It was in a shallow puddle with gas mixed on its surface that created a little rainbow burst like a living painting of a tiny supernova. He picked up the thing and walked the rest of the way back to the car. "69?" He heard a voice call from across the way. *Fuck off,* he didn't look back. He kept walking to the car and opened the big steel door and got in. He reached over to the glovebox and got out some napkins to dry off the little thing and also some electrical tape that he knew had been in there. The tape was gooey from the heat but it would do the trick. He rolled a bit in his fingers, cleaned off the base of the trinket, stuck the tape to the base and then stuck the trinket to the dashboard.

It was a little plastic figurine; something that stuck to a dashboard most likely; the underside was still sticky from where another adhesive had been. It had likely fallen out of another car. It was a little blue man with golden robes sitting cross-legged on a round base. It was a sort of bobble-head. Not so cartoonish as the big novelty ones like they make for athletes and such, but there was a spring there attaching the head giving a bit of a wobble to it. It was some kind of Eastern deity or religious Godhead, obviously. Of course Francis hadn't a clue as to what it was but he was curious about this neat little thing he had just found. It was now stuck on the dash which was hot as hell along with the rest of the car from sitting in a thin column of light through the gas pump and the veranda. The pleather seats seared him through his clothes and the armrest seared the bare skin of his arm. He needed to get moving quickly to get some air passing through and get the trapped heat out of that oven. He hoped the glue from the hot electrical tape and the hot dashboard would hold for his newly acquired friend. He pulled out of the parking lot of the gas station with the head of his little blue partner bouncing excitedly.

Francis pulled out on the cross street from which he'd entered so that he could turn left at the light and continue on his way. The traffic seemed lighter as he waited for his advanced left. He admired his newly acquired passenger, his head now static; motionless; staring; a pursed grin adorning his face. He was holding something like a stick or a flute or something. There wasn't time to get more acquainted as the light turned green and Francis moved through the turn. The moment Francis straightened on the two lane street his stomach sank for a second time and he heard, like a trumpet of Jericho, the screeching belch of that conspicuous monstrosity. He had been stalked like an ignorant rabbit. In his mirror, the grey, dented, lowered, tinted, abominable mess of Bobbi Jones' poor Honda accosted his bumper. He had come straight through the lights where Francis had turned. It couldn't've bothered Francis more than for that man to appear at that time in that place. Bobbi had more horsepower than brains, and that is not to say that Honda had any semblance of impressive horsepower. Whether Francis did or not, Bobbi was going to race him. As soon as things were squared he was going to go; in hopes that Francis would bite; Francis knew this. And whether he wanted it or not, he was sure the guys at work would be talking about it one way or another when he returned. Francis' passenger windows were rolled up, thank God. He'd forgotten to roll them down when he stopped for gas but he was elated they were up now. Ahead of Francis there was a lane closed for street parking. It would occasionally open up into two open lanes for stretches. When it opened Bobbi rushed up beside Francis. Francis stayed in the left lane to avoid talking to him. He didn't want to talk to him – even look at him. So he stared straight ahead even though he knew Bobbi knew he was aware he was there. Eventually, there was no avoiding it and he gave a dismissive wave. *That unibrowed-ass motherfucker*. Bobbi was forced to pull in behind for a moment but again when the lanes opened he again pulled up beside him; head out his window and he was yelling something, Francis couldn't hear what he was saying. *Moron*. He wasn't that terrible guy, Bobbi. But Francis just didn't get this infatuation of economy-turned-"race car"-fad. Bobbi pounded it to pull ahead of Francis as the lane cut down again on account of the parked cars. Francis could see his array of stickers decorating his rear window. Mostly aftermarket parts companies, though that was a presumption as he didn't recognize any. Some stickers were pretty inappropriate (Francis hated seeing that kind of stuff on cars; having kids trying to make sense of that kind of thing; it was gross in his eyes; completely classless and he absolutely loathed it, though he saw that kind of stuff on more than a few cars out there). There was a couple that Francis couldn't make sense of either way. Like the big blue 2D shark decal in the top left of the window. It said *shovel-head* across it and Francis thought, *yeah that's about right*. The two puttered along in traffic all the while Bobbi revving the ever-loving-shit out of his poor little Honda. Just a through-and-through imbecile.

The sound reverberated off the flat walls of the buildings. Oh, did Francis ever want him to piss off. But he knew that just wouldn't happen. Deep down Francis suspected that Bobbi was immensely jealous of his Coronet, though Bobbi would never admit it. "It's not even a Super bee," he'd cackle. *Not even a car that never was.* That burned Francis. As if that fat-sack-of-shit had a fraction of anything as nice as that in his life. Francis put a lot of money into that car after he'd said that at work one day a couple summers ago. Bobbi acted like muscle cars should be a bygone notion. As ancient as the dinosaur. Just forget those beasts as if they never happened. Old inefficient relics; it was a point of comedy to him. Francis didn't know if he could get behind that. Not that he thought of them as a pinnacle of achievement or something to put up on a pillar, but actively not acknowledging where something came from, its historical roots, whatever, was just outright sinful. Bobbi would mock everything about them; the absurd gigantism, the heaviness, the pointless grandeur of them all. Anything he could needle at, he did. Though it was all a thin veil for his jealousy and Francis knew it. He looked up ahead and the line of parked cars to the right of him was ending. When it opened up Bobbi veered hard right to the now open lane. There was a traffic light about to turn yellow. Beyond was a long stretch of two open lanes. This would be it. Francis crept to the stop bar as a man shuffles his feet on his way to the electric chair. Again, Bobbi was yelling something and again Francis couldn't hear but he didn't need to. He knew what was happening. The three-eighty-three chugged roughly, unaware of its impending labours. Francis watched the walk hand as it switched from the white walk-man to the orange stop hand that counted down below it. *Fourteen seconds*. He watched the traffic speed through the intersection to make the light that would be soon changing to yellow. He scanned the intersection quickly for any police that may be around. He watched the people walking on the sidewalk going about their business. *Frig*, did he not want to do this. He thought about turning left and getting out of there but he knew this wouldn't be the last time he'd be tormented by that oaf. He looked at his little blue friend who, to his surprise, was nodding; shaking his head up and down feverishly. *Three seconds*. He looked over at Bobbi Jones; he was intensely focused, looking down the field. The cross street light went yellow and Francis held his breath. He gripped the thin wheel and Hurst shifter with the nervous energy like a needle in the mouth before a dental freezing. His legs were stiff in ready anticipation. The left ready to dump the clutch; he released the brake with the other and hovered it over the gas. The car lurched slightly, revealing his intentions now without a doubt. The light went green. Bobbi fired off like a loosed slingshot which surprised Francis. Bobbi's car was loud; quite obnoxiously loud, but Francis had heard that sound often enough. Leaving work almost every day Bobbi would mat it; that was just how he drove everywhere. Even the people on the sidewalk were fairly accustomed to guys like Bobbi screaming around town here and there and hardly took notice; a minor annoyance to most people. It took a fraction of a fraction of a second, though it seemed like a full minute compared to Bobbi's lightweight, fuel injected Honda, for the Coronet to suck in the air and the fuel demanded by the wide open throttle; like an athlete filling his lungs before an action. The sound which erupted from the fifty year old Coronet was not accustomed to by the ears of the city's twenty first century pedestrians. Francis could see the heads snap around to see the spectacle. He was sure they didn't appreciate it, but whether they liked it or not it was a spectacle. Like a lion fighting a hyena in the street would command attention, one couldn't help but look. Bobbi got good grip off his start and he slowly slammed through to second gear. Francis' tires broke loose off the line. He had no choice but to lift a little only to see Bobbi pull a little further ahead. When Francis felt comfortable his traction returned he rolled into it and could then feel the secondaries open up and he got that familiar feeling he'd felt while bombing around country roads. It was a strange feeling that felt almost as if the car was floating. Francis had felt it before when that car was pushed beyond its comfortable limit it acted like it had a desire of its own. As if it was acting just a little bit past the point of control. Just past the edge. Like a Bull Mastiff pulling someone on rollerblades. The wheel felt just a little looser; the front tires just a little less responsive; it drifted whichever way it wanted; it floated around on its own whim. The big engine began to beat its chest as Francis disregarded the ire of the onlookers and focused on the field; the drag strip he now found himself on. Bobbi's lead was eaten up and then it was no more. The wide open Coronet resonated off the buildings and through alleyways. The thrashing violence of it all was fully on display. There wasn't a person within thirty blocks that didn't know what was going on. Least especially was the unmarked SUV that had its lights already blazing as Bobbi and Francis were flying through an intersection. It flew by in a flash but Francis, and no doubt Bobbi too, could see that the SUV was two or three cars back in line at an intersecting light and was beginning to pull around the stopped cars as the two raced by. He would be on their asses in a minute. But they had a decent lead on him and it was one car against two. Francis was not in the mood to get in complete shit from, as far as he was concerned, Bobbi Jones' moronic idea. And he knew that idiot wouldn't be quick to concede.

Francis could see up ahead that the exhibition was over. There were cars stopped at solid red. He was satisfied he had pulled on Bobbi and got on the brakes hard. If there was an Achilles heel to that Coronet it was its manual drum brakes. One of the rear wheels locked up, Francis got on them so hard. The cars in front were coming up fast and so too was the SUV from behind. Bobbi came flashing up to the Coronet and pulled in behind of Francis in his lane, stopping with more ease than the Coronet could behind the car stopped at the light with Francis narrowly skidding to a halt behind it. He didn't know what Bobbi's plan was; if he hadn't seen the cop there all the better, but he must have seen him by now flying up behind them and Francis was sure Bobbi was now feverishly thinking of a way to evade him. They were at the highway that traversed overhead just in front of them. The lights they were stopping for was a road that was partly an onramp for that highway and which you could also go straight through an underpass of the highway. You couldn't turn left immediately unless you first went under the overpass. He checked his mirror and the red and blue strobes were about three or four blocks back and coming quick. The light showed no signs of changing and Francis was desperate. He noticed that the curb of the street to his right had a depression which he knew Bobbi couldn't see as the large back end of the Coronet blinded him from it. Francis waited until the cop was close so that Bobbi wouldn't have time to react. He then turned and straddled the sidewalk like an 80's action movie and got around stopped cars in front of him. He wasn't sure why the car at the stop line was just sitting there in the turn lane. He gave a quick glance to the passing traffic which was fast and busy. It was a one-way street but it was about four lanes wide, and he had to immediately get across all four and hammer it to merge onto the highway. As soon as there was even the slightest gap in cars Francis nudged out and unceremoniously crossed the four lanes causing virtually everyone on the road to brake and barrage him with a bevy of honks and jeers. As far as he could tell there were no sounds of crunching metal or breaking glass so he punched it and again ripped his way up the ramp and onto the highway. He tried his best to look in the small mirrors for the police car or to see what Bobbi did while also trying to merge onto the busy highway. He couldn't see anything a few hundred feet after he crested the ramp and he couldn't hear anything over the roar of his own car and whirl of the highway. He kept glancing at his mirror waiting for blue and red lights to come screaming up the ramp at which point he would be royally fucked, but after a bit of distance there was nothing so he decided to settle in and do his best to camouflage into the mass of grey, white and black vehicles that corralled down the highway.

In an instant he was surrounded by the disorienting herd that buzzed and sped at a bewildering rate eastward; away from the home of Beatrice. A steel stampede; a flock of molded metal. He kept pace and did his best to blend in; hiding among the crowd. He was no one here; no one along with the rest of the crowd; just an ordinary citizen. There was everything in the crowd of vehicles: Versa's, Jetta's, cab drivers Impalas, the throaty exhaust of a second gen Ram matting it for seemingly no reason, a Harley doing likewise; because they could, he supposed. All the sound annoyed him (and yes, he was aware he was a contributor to that cacophony). They were all grey, white and black. He couldn't find one that wasn't one of those colours. He couldn't find a reason for them all to be that way. But they were. To him, they were all soulless appliances.

With only the driver window down there was an intolerable pulsing of air throughout the car which aggravated his ears adding to his agony. He checked his mirror again for any sign of trouble. He was well on his way at this point. Certainly now, Bobbi would have got the sour end of the deal, he figured. *That ogre can have it.* Rife with anxiety he turned on the radio and pushed through the big mechanical buttons of the pre-set stations then finely dialing them the rest of the way to get the strongest signal. Francis was no one, going nowhere. There was a whole lot of nothing he could find on the radio until finally he settled on something dreadfully upbeat.

The adrenaline of the event eventually wore down, although he remained anxious and felt that any and all other police in the city would be after him. It was trumped up in his mind most likely, but he couldn't be quite sure. The excitement before the highway was shortly contrasted thereafter by more monotonous stopping and going of near gridlock traffic again. Francis wasn't quite sure he could tolerate any more of that. Eventually he had to turn around. The best way to get back on track to Beatrice's would be to get off the highway and get right back on going the other way. The traffic was dense even in the middle of the day. He had wriggled over three lanes from any of the approaching off-ramps and because of this, he decided that aggressively merging towards any of those offramps into the quagmire of neighbourhood he was near, and their labyrinth-like routes of one-way streets and dead-ends to turnaround, wasn't something that particularly interested him. He knew that neighbourhood and it was not fun to drive around in, nor was it as simple as making three left turns and heading back the other way. He'd slug it out and turn around at an exit further down. It was a bit of a jaunt but it was worth the ease of simplicity. Traffic going the other way seemed to be moving fine. His phone had slid on the floor at some point so he had no idea if Betty had messaged him back yet. He made a half-hearted attempt to look for it by feeling around for it in the slow traffic but he couldn't grasp it. He kept a constant eye on the car in front of him. The Mercedes he'd smashed into the back of under similar circumstances about a decade prior when he'd first got his license was flashing to him in vivid recall. Stopping and going; more stopping than going. Every other lane than his was quicker, of course. The pace picked up as he watched another off-ramp pass by.

Just as traffic began to flow Francis moved over and hit the off ramp and realized he was close to a part of town that had a mom-and-pop hunting store that he liked. He wanted to grab a little hunting doo-dad he'd been thinking about lately even though deer season was months away. He figured he wouldn't be around here again for some time. When he parked he searched for his phone on the floor of the car and had seemingly vanished in the bedlam. He found it after some difficulty and when he checked it he revealed a melee of messages from Beatrice.

You dont have to worry
aboutme anymore
Dont come over
its fine
Im fine
I think Im going to kill myself today
So youll finally be rid of me.
I wont bother you anymore

The heat reflected off the beige stucco wall of the store as well as up from the vast expanse of the great, barren parking lot that Francis had pulled into. Other than Francis and the Coronet, there were only two other cars parked on the periphery of the lot that could easily hold hundreds of vehicles. There was a lifeless tree in the middle of that vast space; perched up in some cold concrete planters box; a horrid attempt, at one time, to try and inject beauty into a lost cause of a space. It was a desert in half an acre; if it was half an acre. Francis' mouth was dry and his lips stuck together like tape being peeled off a roll. His throat was so dry that it felt like cactus needles were growing out of the walls of it. He could use a water or a Gatorade. There was a gas station up the street a-ways. He should have got one when he stopped for gas earlier. As he sat there in the now undeniable mid-day heat, prickle throated and cotton-mouthed, his attention was drawn to the dark propped-open doorway across the asphalt desert. From that little dark opening came a faint low sound that pulsed like a heartbeat. It was the mechanical rhythm of unintelligible dance music. It was an establishment which he'd been to a time or two before with his buddies for whatever reason they happened to drum up on that particular night. He could go in there for a beer, maybe. One or two to bring the blood pressure down a touch. He once heard a story from a woman that she was given a beer to calm herself down after her first born in the hospital; she was having trouble breastfeeding; too stressed, supposedly. Anyway, the nurse gave her a beer to chill out. He didn't know why he thought of that just then but he supposed the likeness to his situation was sound enough and he made his way across the parking lot thinking about it. *They certainly don't do that kind of thing anymore,* he thought. Well, it probably wasn't proper practice at the time either so who knows? He walked through the door in an almost trance-like state; a thirsty, desert-wanderer from antique lands. And, except for the command to doff his hat by the doorman, he slipped unhindered into the dark space of black lights, strobe flashes and neon colours. The muted rumbling from the parking lot became a palpable and uncomfortable blast felt throughout the body once he passed the threshold. The trance was snapped when he was about five paces into the large room. Suddenly, it was as if Francis walked across the stage itself. All eyes in that room were fixed upon him. The bartender, the hostess, the girl on stage languidly toeing around and the two rough looking guys that sat together at one small table at the side. That was all that occupied that large room, although, Francis got the sensation that there were a few more peering eyes in a corner or lurking on a catwalk somewhere high above him, but he didn't look around to find out. He knew in an instant that he had made a mistake. *Fuck. Ah fuck*, he thought. *What the fuck are you doing in here?* He couldn't turn around now; he couldn't. He didn't know what he'd expected exactly. It was precisely what you would expect on an idle, early, weekday afternoon. He hadn't thought about it before he walked across the parking lot; he'd just done it. Better to get on with something like that than to mull it over too much he found from past experience. But once inside there, only paces in, he realized what an unconscionable error he'd made. He thought about turning around and heading straight out; getting some phantom phony phone call or feigning that he forgot something in his car. *Yeah, how phony that would be,* he thought. What would it matter anyway? Absolutely nothing to anyone. But no, he'd go and sit down and get his beer he so desperately needed. He walked fast, but not too fast, and sat down at the row of small tables along a wall far from the stage. He sat there quietly radiating anxiety like an exposed nuclear reactor core.

The song ended and the girl on stage walked measuredly up the steel stairs and vanished into a dressing room. The server came over and asked if she could start him off with a drink and if he'd be eating. *What the fuck?* thought Francis. He ordered a quart because that was apparently all they served and told the server no to the latter. The door from which he entered was right over there; just as far as when he walked in. No one would think anything of it. No one would give a shit. But now he'd ordered a beer and was shackled to it. She came back with the quart. He paid by credit and hoped it wouldn't get declined. He'd get out of there as soon as that beer was done. He started drinking it fast. It was good; there was that at least. A voice came on the speaker and welcomed the next dancer onto the stage. She hadn't come down the steel stairs before two women came over to Francis. They had been sitting in a booth where he couldn't see them when he walked in. They walked over slowly, as if the place was full of people. It seemed that that was the only speed that they knew. One sat in the empty chair across the table and the other sat on his knee. This was like watching a movie scene play out that he'd seen a dozen times before. He had never been to a strip club alone. And never in the middle of the afternoon. He felt like a coyote with a leg stuck in a trap; or one stuck on his knee for that matter. The woman on his knee asked what his name was, to which he said most incredulously, uh Matt. He didn't know why he said that. It didn't matter; she couldn't have given one iota of a shit. He could have said President Eisenhower and it wouldn't have mattered. But she liked that name, go figure. She introduced herself and her friend, to which Francis smiled cordially. He felt like an ass; and he was. She asked if it was his first time here and that she'd never seen him before. *Yes, this was his first time. This is the birth of a regular.* He retorted that he'd been here before. *Ass.* She asked promptly if he wanted to go upstairs? *Buy me a drink first,* he thought. She was French - Montreal French. You must want to go upstairs with her, the seated woman asked. Franicis told her maybe in a bit and that he was waiting for someone. She suggested that her friend could stay here and let Francis' friend know that they were upstairs, and that they would be quick, all of which Francis hoped sounded just as absurd to her as it did to him so he just stared at her until he could politely decline once again. He eventually mustered enough within himself to ask her what her name was. It was Cercé. He didn't hear what the seated girl's name was. Francis said something to the effect of how epic that was. She didn't hear him properly and said, no like the Game of Thrones, you know? The music was loud. Francis asked if her mother named her Cercé? She giggled conceitedly and looked towards the ceiling. The unspoken truths buzzed in and out of them, never occurring to either the kaleidoscopic story of each other that lay under a thin veil of ragged cordiality. The business was anonymity. And both, in their own ways, understood the business. She asked if Francis could buy them a drink. He said perhaps when his friend got there. Francis mustered up another lie: he had to go to the bathroom. Cercé slid off his lap. Francis got up and walked briskly and pointedly. He heard someone behind him shout about it being the other way, but with his first resolute steps let everyone; the two rough gentlemen; the two dancers; the DJ and the doorman, know where he was going. *What the hell?* He walked out through that small dark vestibule and into the searing heat of the barren parking lot. Light refracted off every surface and focused on Francis like light through a magnifying glass. He walked the long walk back across the pale grey asphalt to the Coronet and past the tree that was there. The tree had four or five leaves; he hadn't noticed that before. He thought it had no leaves, but he couldn't remember. He got to his car, got in, and closed the door. When he was in the car he could still smell the club; he could still smell "Cercé." *Fuck*, he fumed. He used to have an old t-shirt in the back seat or on the floor somewhere in the car but he knew he had taken that out the other week when he cleaned the car. The only thing resembling a change of clothes was a fluorescent vest of his from work. He supposed he could scoot home again now to change, since he was way away from where he should be. It'd be less difficult to get there than to try and go back to Betty's. Traffic westbound at this point in the day would be starting to get bananas anyway, he thought to himself. He'd do just as well to go back that way and retrace his steps than to hop back on the highway and slug it out in the opposite direction. He checked his hat then put it on and looked in the mirror. For reasons unknown he was in this parking lot. For beer, he supposed. He looked around and noticed the hunting store he'd forgotten all about. *Frig, oh well, I got to get out of here.* He turned the key to start his car and *quaquaquaqua. Holy fuck what was that?* he thought. A rattling sound from under the hood violently disturbed the quiet hiss of the hot parking lot. There was something wrong with the car. For reasons unknown some senseless thing was beating some other poor senseless thing into abominable oblivion. He shut the car off, got out and opened the hood. The air cleaner was off and laying wedged between the motor and the fender skirt. The fan looked like it might have given it a few decent whacks before he shut the motor off. It had a minor dent and the filter was a bit torn but not all the way through.. The threaded rod that held the cleaner to the carburetor, for reasons unknown, had broken off. That pretty much sealed the deal right there; he'd slip home before heading once more to Betty's. He could patch that up and grab a shirt there. He grabbed the air cleaner and threw it on the bench seat beside him as he climbed in again. He was not thrilled about driving around without an air filter on but that's how it was for now. He tried the ignition again to *quaquaquaqua.* The car did not start. The car should start. An air cleaner coming off is no reason to stop a car from starting. *Think!* For reasons unknown it would not start. *Please God allow this car to start,* he thought. *Quaquaqua. Vapor-lock?* He flicked the switch for the inline electric fuel pump he and Drake installed while attempting to sort out some fuel problems last summer. He ran it for about ten seconds and tried again. The car started. Lana Del Rey was playing on the radio and that was ok; he liked her stuff. He looked around that wasteland to nothing. He looked at his sweaty face in the rear view mirror. For now the car idled there, blowing hot air at Francis from the dash vent. *Well, shall we go? Yes, let's go.*

He tossed his phone on the bench seat between himself and the air cleaner. The screen flashed its blank impassive face; divine athambia from the cold dark thing. It had been about an hour since he'd heard from Beatrice which was something he could hardly believe. He was aware he didn't message her back, but still. He hadn't heard very much from her over the last week at all. It was always him starting a conversation off or checking in on her. Conversations often about as reciprocal as a fallen tree. She was somehow always due for an empathetic ear. Unless everything was "fine," which was way more work to Francis than just listening to out-and-out complaining. He thought they had been a good team, but now he wasn't sure. *If they say the world was built for two, then I ought to be thy Adam,* he thought. He looked at that tree. *What about hanging myself?* He looked at his phone. It would give him an erection. *You sick fuck. You're a monster.* How could one think of these things at such a time? He didn't know what to think as he pointed his car towards home. He shut his mind off; just drove in divine apathia.

He thought again about those dreaded dull, dead-fish-eyed people offering their uncomfortable, questionably sincere, condolences in his inevitable return to work. They didn't know his dad; they didn't really know him. Francis was stiff from the thought of that cold office space where he would get his orders in the morning before he left with his bag of tools and his lead-hand for the day; the same as every other day. The rigamortis he felt now as he drove home thinking about it. He'd feel that way the day he'd return as well; probably even much worse. He feared the feeling would be permanent. One day off paid; one day off not; it is imperative that you return your shoulder to the wheel. That was that. Return to life.

Home was a funny way of thinking about that house. It was a house now. He drove the long way back to the house not thinking of much. Only the air and light and time and space of that little apartment he'd have one day on the other side of town. Where he could write and toil on his projects. Finally, he'd have the time. Alone and sad and perfect and fuelled by black coffee and a lack of sleep; maybe he'd take up smoking; sweating profusely in the hot space, bleeding over a typewriter or laptop or whatever; break a bone in his hand after he'd punch something when he would inevitably fail and give up. He pulled into the driveway of the house and up to the garage. He sat for a minute but it was too hot so he got out and got to fixing the air cleaner. The threaded rod that held it down had sheared off. He rummaged around the garage for a bit and found a long bolt that would suffice in replacing it. Thank God the other half of the rod didn't walk out and fall down into the air intake; it was easy enough to spin out. The whole thing took only a few minutes. He went inside the empty house and grabbed a glass of water. His feet were hot from his boots so he slid them off and went to the bathroom tub and ran them under cold water. He had athletes' foot, so he tried to cool them down as best he could whenever they got too hot for too long. It was a losing game. When he got done he put on new socks, then the same old boots that were still hot in the soles and went outside and got back in the car. He backed it up out onto the street and headed back towards Betty's without much thought. The same way as the first time but with more jam this time. It was the best way. The faster he drove the more pleasant the drive was. The time for listlessness had passed. It'd soon be getting close to around supper time. He didn't think he had eaten anything all day. Except for coffee and the neck of a beer if you count those. Maybe Betty and he could go out for something. Though he knew it'd take a fair amount of arm-twisting to get her out of the house even though he knew deep down she'd want to grab a burger or something. He drove through the city mostly the same as before, though without even bothering testing his luck with the bridge construction this time. Enduring more monotony for the hundredth time in one day. It felt as though it'd been ten hours since he and Beatrice first messaged in the morning. It wasn't.

She was beautiful, she was. All the time. Even in those moments that she shouldn't have been. Those idle Monday nights in sweatpants and no makeup at the tail ends of days; she was beautiful. A natural beauty that her best friend's mother cheerfully lauded her for; to the chagrin of her own daughter, Francis recalled. All in good spirit, but it was true.

I think we should go out tonight

He could see her now twisting a lilac stalk in her hand

I think we should talk

> *But this is what I mean.*
> *We should watch a sunset*
> *tonight or something.*

What? What are you
talking about?
I don't want to
do anything.

> *That's not what I meant at all*
> *That is not what I meant at all*
> *Like, a sunset you know?*
> *Let us go then*
> *you and I with the*
> *evening spread*
> *out against the sky?*

No. You don't
get it do you?

She kills me, he thought. She has become death, the
destroyer of words.

He shouldn't have said that. He was being a bit of an ass, but he didn't really know what to say. What could he say that he hadn't said before? He loved her; he did. But *Jesus Christ* was it work at times. He was no saint. He had a fair amount of tolerance for her and her shit, but when Francis flew off the handle it was a train-derailed. He could recall in vivid detail a particular time when he lost it good, which he was lamenting over now as he drove. He was on the phone with his mother, pacing in the backyard; his escape to solace at the time; and she was losing her absolute shit over him cooking fish-sticks in the oven or something or other. She was losing it; screaming at him from the back deck for the entire quaint, peaceful small town to hear. There was more to it than the fish, for that he was sure. There was a deep-seated resentment for who was on the other end of the line, for one thing. He knew it but he couldn't figure out how to solve it. Though he was trying like a bastard. She was dealing with her shit in her own way, albeit, piss-poorly if you asked Francis. Though she did it often, it tasked him, still. He remembered when he got off the phone was when he snapped. Her, shielding herself under the barbaric blows of a flaccid oven mitt like a petrified mouse under the murderous thrashing of claw and tooth. The raining blows fell from a frustrated caveman; composed no longer, unbridled his finest hour in thirty excruciating seconds. You can't help memories like that from coming back. He thought about that often.

He figured he should be able to get fifteen thousand for the Coronet at minimum; that's close to a year's rent. He could probably get a full year's rent, he was just being conservative. Even though the car was far from a showpiece those Mopars continued their skyrocketing rise in price. He knew the second he'd post it he'd have offers galore. He looked to the little blue figure riding his dashboard and asked it if it had any ideas. It was static; burning there in the heat it found itself in. *I should have the right to my work; the right to try and make it work,* he thought. Maybe he should just be more sensible. The world doesn't need any more Bukowski's; the man said so himself.

His drive back flowed through certain half-deserted streets, leading him to an overwhelming nothing. Francis saw strange people lounging in a park as he passed by. He saw bluebirds bursting out from them up to the nearby birches. He saw a certain old man sitting on a certain bench in a certain way which made him take a second glance; a cornet being played among friends of some two or three; a madman shaking a dead geranium. An uncomfortable apathy coursed through him and he stared at the road coming at him like a conveyor belt. He felt inside his brain a dull tom-tom begin. He felt a feeling one feels as one passes a piano, unplayed; not even tickling it as one walks by. Silence as he drove along. To Francis, nothing beside him remained but the birches bent to left and right by means unknown; but one can dream. He thought a bit about those birches; now peppered with bluebirds. Some of them were bent down permanently; some of them broken altogether; they'd never be righted again. On others there was the play of shine and shade on them as the supple boughs wag. He thought for a minute that he might like to climb one while there are still some in fine enough shape to climb. And then there were the leaves of grass which Francis saw which no one else seemed to see. The grass here which was shore down; too short if you asked him. Francis continued on down the street. What more could he do?

He passed a church in a desolate place. It was alone along the road. The great olive doors were shut as they were always shut on churches, he found; they all seemed to be that way. It was a great church though, it looked a bit like the Notre Dame Cathedral. It was a museum. *Should I go in and look around? A rich sight that'd be.* In the glow of the beautiful stained glass light, under the watch of the solemn statue of St. Francis of Assisi, a pathetic sight of a feeble, gnarled back slug in Carhartt pants and work boots leaving its slimy trail in and abruptly out. He couldn't walk in there. He preferred to stay in the car and roll by slowly trying to catch a glimpse should its doors open for a second.

Thinking about it was good enough for him. Religion when he dies. But he would really like to take a good look around inside. He often wondered about the insides of those churches. This one looked unreal.

I should just walk in; act like I've been there a hundred times. What does that stained glass look like; the murals of the trials of Christ? It's a museum, he thought. It would be dead inside. He knew it was dead inside. No one should, less a desperate priest, God forbid – *God forbid*, come up and talk to him. *Dear God*, he thought, *if that happened...he couldn't.* He didn't know what he'd do then. Wanting to know what the hell he was doing in there? Wouldn't they both like to know. *I think I'd feel more comfortable with Cercé on my lap.* He didn't know jack about anything in there. Just the big stuff he knew. But no one would be certain of anything any more than he would in there either, really. The really big stuff, he meant. What was the point? He wouldn't want anyone to have to clean his slimy slug trail; a roadmap of every step he's taken; every inch accounted for; all around like a traveled road map that his dusty work boots would leave on that marble floor. He got it. Try not to be an asshole and try to leave things in better shape than when you found them. That's all there is to it. Surely if he went in there a priest would catch him in conversation. He'd be a pointless bother to anyone in there. He remained outside in his car. It wasn't a museum; he was a fool. He craned his neck down so that he could look up through the windshield to see the big church in its entirety as best he could. He was looking for butterflies on the arches of that grey gothic exterior. *Nothing*, he thought.

He'd drift in and out of his fog of thinking and, at last, unceremoniously turned down the street on which Beatrice, his love, lived. He was there, finally. He'd go in and talk to her and probably stay all evening long; maybe the night. He parked along the street in front of her house. The place she rented was the basement unit of a house that was owned and occupied upstairs by a fairly nice older Greek gentleman. *I'm here*, he texted her. Her place could hardly be seen from the street. It was blocked from view by a hedgerow of gnarled mess. Mostly scrubby cedar shrubs which permitted pervasive climbing vines that ran through it like veins. The hole through the green wall that led up the walkway to the cement stoop was overgrown so that one could hardly pass through without being accosted by the clutching and grappling of plants on your clothes. He passed through to the depressing yard that was choked from sunlight by the tall maples that stood quietly at the sides of the enclosed front lawn. More dirt than lawn; more like a forest floor with the amount of dead cedar needles. Black birds perched atop the hardwood trees observed his entry to this space. An audacious few questioned his presence there as he paced by. One took to flight and cried a warning: jug jug jug jug. Francis entered through the screened in porch and once into the house he darted down the stairs to the right then descended to the basement. He was expecting to see Beatrice there as he'd seen her often before: sprawled out, in deep sleep on the bed; television blasting that could wake the dead, if not her. But, she was not there. The apartment was empty, cold and unwelcoming. "Well-lived in," would be a diplomatic way of putting it. Clothes made up the flooring and furniture coverings; dirty, clean, who could tell? Bags of every sort from reusable shopping bags to a purse and tote bags filled with God-knows-what were interspersed throughout the array of varying states of laundry piles. A vacuum, some mops and brooms leaned where they pleased. There was nothing close to anything resembling any type of order here. Not even an attempt made at order. There were so many bags everywhere. Some were filled with more clothes, others had groceries that never made it to their destination in a pantry. Many others were filled with garbage to go out but also hadn't yet made it there. The apartment itself was essentially a long single room with a little unofficial kitchenette installed on the far side, a little futon with a TV on a small table could be considered a living room area which sat in front of a bed and another smaller tv on the nightstand. That TV was on and blasting deafeningly to no one. There was no Beatrice. Her bed was not made, which was ordinary. The sheets were damp but cold. They were damp because her medication made her sweat like she showered on the bed. He sat down on the other side of the bed and thought for a minute what to do. He looked at his phone and there was nothing new on it. He hadn't heard from Beatrice in hours. Should he wait for her, he thought. Should he leave her a note? A more personal touch, maybe? Proving that he had, in fact, come to see her? He looked around and saw a photo of the two of them that was on a little desk that separated her "bedroom" and her "living room." It was of the two of them a couple of Canada Days ago; one of the first times they'd gone out as an item, he remembered. They were kissing and he was looking at the photographer while she was enthralled with the kiss. It was a cute photo. But Francis remembered that he didn't remember a lot from that day. He couldn't even tell you what bar that picture was taken in. *You do not know how longingly I look upon you.* Where could she have gone? *Anywhere,* he considered. She had a little red Corolla her parents had bought for her which would have been parked around the back of the house. He could see it wasn't in the driveway from the window at the top of the wall that looked out to that rear alley. He was quite sure it was gone. Beatrice would often "take a minute," or an hour or four. She'd drive to some park or parking lot somewhere and cry and text Francis frantically as he'd try and calm her down. It was a familiar old story. She would collect herself and Francis would find out where she was and go to her or she would come home on her own. But she was not texting him back. He looked at his phone again. When was the last time she had texted him? He couldn't remember. It was a while ago anyway. He tried to call her. He looked around, it was a cute apartment if you were used to a prison cell. It had everything you needed, he supposed. It was decorated in the style of every other girl's first apartment: that industrial chic smashed together with Scandinavian bulk gauche. It wasn't that bad actually, it was cute and well done if the clothes were put away. Francis thought about doing that for her, but she'd yelled at him before for messing this or that up or folding something that shouldn't be folded, so whatever. Francis looked on the nightstand and saw a little clock radio, a couple of old pill bottles, water bottles and his little scrape razor of his that he found to be quite perplexing. It was his scrape razor, that there was no doubt. A simple little tool with a handle that had interchangeable razor blades used to scrape gunk off stuff. Francis hadn't brought it over here. It was definitely his, he could tell. But it should have been at his place among his stuff. He racked his memory to try and recall if he had brought it over for a job or something but he was sure he hadn't. Why was this here, he thought?

Then like a thousand swords piercing his heart and lungs at once, his breath was gone from him as he understood why. Suddenly, the scene unveiled itself to Francis. A great turmoil had occurred here like the sparring of two bucks fighting on a forest floor; upturning the leaves, roots and soil as the duvet was now. This had happened before; Francis knew it; he was not naive. But he'd never seen it in such cold contemplation before. Such frankness; such earnestness; complete lucidity. Right there on the fucking table sat still the simple little death machine. His stomach was on the verge of being undone. He felt sick.

I'm fine

Jesus, he could breathe.

I don't think you are

*I don't want to go
on like this.*

*I'm not going to pretend like
I know what you're going*

through Bea. But I'd like
to help you get through it.

You'll be done with me soon.
And then you can go on
and have a nice life
and forget all about me.
Get married and have
kids and start a new life
and forget me.

Well that's not true.
I would never forget you.
And doing what you're
thinking isn't a solution.
You know that.
We've talked about this before.

I can't even do basic fucking
things in life.
I can't even make an
appointemnt like I should
I need to make a doctors
appointment and I
need to get in to see a psych
AGAIIN>
these meds arn't working
im going to stop taking them.

I don't know what to do.

I'm not a doctor.
But it seems to me
like the doctors have
been striking out for you for years.
Like how many med
changes have you been on?

Like in my whole life?
I can't even
ducking count. Since I was 14.
I've told you that

I wouldn't argue with
you if you want to try
clean living out for a
while and see how that goes.
You know what I mean.

Ya

I'd be worried about
the affects of the
other stuff you do though too.
Like try it really clean
I mean.

Ya you've talked about
that before.
I fucking know.
Weed doesn't effect me like that.

*Well you know
how I feel about it.*

*Ya your fucking "studies."
Do you think I want
to smoke forever?
I fucking don't ok?
But it's the only thing
that gets me through the day.*

Ya I know.

*I just want it to be over.
I'm done with this.*

*Where are you?
I'm at your place right now.
Are you close?*

I went for a drive.

Are you still driving?

*No I'm just taking a minute.
I'll come home
when I'm ready.*

*Ok well I don't want
you passing out*

102

like last time and
spending the night
out in your car somewhere.

I wont.

Well just tell me where you
are and I'll come to you.

It's fine.
I want to be alone.

I guess I'll just drive
around until I
find you then.

Fine. Suit yourself.

B. Come on

Who could fathom a more paralyzing force in this world? Both in their own way. Frozen waist deep down in this hellish basement, Francis certainly felt paralyzed. He could not move. For a long while he just sat there feeling like an asshole. He couldn't contemplate what Bety was truly feeling.

Well, there was nothing to do now but to go find her. So he got up from the bedside, nauseous and uneasy he wavered up the stairs. Each step tasked his legs that had that gelatinous exhausted quivering to them. It felt like he had just run a marathon while simultaneously feeling like it was the first time he'd ever walked on them. Out of the house he passed the clawing and thrashing of the overgrown vegetation. The hardwoods moaned in the harassing wind. He opened the door to the car and got in and started the machine. In moments he would learn that upon closing the door he would have taken with him a thorned branch of climbing vine which would be pinched in the weatherstripping of the Coronet. And, upon driving away those branches would cut his head as they tightened and pulled their way through the door seam with ungodly might. He saw his cut head in the rear view mirror. He put his hat on that'd been on the dash the salt from which stung his head for a moment.

The noise from the radio battered him. There was an assaulting commercial which pervaded his senses like a sinus cold. *Christ, stop trying to get me into a new Toyota.* It was just an obnoxious unrelenting barrage on the senses; one of the many omnipresent advertisements out there. His heartburn tightened his chest. Like nails on a chalkboard; like nails being driven into ears; fingernails being raked over eyelids. Music as soothing as an air hammer; louder than a morning alarm after a sleepless night; more jarring than the best laid words of poets, long dead, taken all wrong. He didn't think he could have hated anything more in the world at that particular moment than 'ZERO DOWN, ON APPROVED CREDIT.'

There were about three places she would most likely be, he figured. Francis drove slowly and indiscriminately down the street, checking aimlessly in this corner or that; or this lot or alley or shoulder of the road here or there. He was hoping to get a message from Beatrice that would bring him to the edge of the city or to the edge of civilization itself, he didn't care. He subconsciously meandered north towards the river. He was heading towards one of the city parks abutting the riverbank; one of the places he'd found her before. But maybe he would just hop on the parkway and cross the river when he got near there and drive over the Hills and keep on going. Up to La Pêche or Gracefield or maybe further; maybe way further. That thought was just moronic, *stop*. He could recall in vivid detail a friend of his once share with him his asinine plan, *Northern Quebec, bud; they'll never find you in Northern Quebec*. He could also hop on the highway and take the fast way back south and out of the city. He'd throw his phone out the window and be done with it, *just fuck...* Fuck was he ever so close to joining the Air Force. He wouldn't have had to deal with this shit. His little blue figurine friend bobbed his little blue head. He hardly knew this little thing. He might end up back in that rainbow puddle where he came from if he kept up like that...*Little Fuck*. But Francis knew enough to know. *For fuck's sake*.

He drove around in silence. He went through small narrow streets and out onto larger arteries then back again. There was nothing he noticed about anything. The opaque periphery was inconsequential to him; there was only the car in front of him and the brake lights and the traffic signs that mattered. In time, he found himself away from the cluster of the city. In a place where the city quiets down in between that and another. "Greenspace" is what they called it. Protected farmland or forest that was not to be developed on. He found himself quite alone there surrounded by nothing, staring at a lonely stop sign.

The great V8 sputtered; the V8 muttered; as though it was in its final gasps of life. Might it die, it would leave him there alone among the abyss of endless fields he now found himself in. He stared down one way to the left and another to the right; there was no straight way to go; a "T" from which two roads diverged. He looked up to the rear view mirror; the many and magnificent artificers staring back and shouting; beckoning; heckling. But through pursed and wrinkled lips and sneer of cold defeat, a dull and diminishing visage returned his gaze, leaving himself a mirage on the hot black road which sliced through those desolate fields. A soft hand caressed the wheel then clenched tight the rein. The heart beat; the car idled; all pulsing like a drum. A dull, persistent tomtom in his mind. Looking down the long flat hood; the compiled work of great and many; the envy of many; the tomtom bled on like a heart beating through an open wound. To his side the low and level fields and hills of beans stretched far away. Further yet, over the mountains of red rock, black, uncertain rain clouds brooded; filling the sky like ink into a water glass. How queer the pull to those red rocks was. Past the fields and plains of mud-cracked earth; to a little chapel on a hill he knew would be there. The dry wind moved the struggling fields. Oh, if there were only rain coming over those red rocks. All the creatures were out at play, if one could stop and listen (and if one could neglect the tomtom in one's head): the cock on the chapel peek, the *jug jug jug jug* overhead; the cicada piercing the ear like a slow and deliberate jab of a spear of grass. *Should I stay here,* he thought? *Should I park my car and I could lean and loafe at my ease here on this roadside? Try and loose the stop from my throat and get to work right here?* Over those distant mountains is my new apartment there? *The seed here which blooms there; a new man?* Dry thunder rumbled high in the heavens, scarce heard amid the void below. To a sober brain, it spoke to him. *That is not the way,* he thought. The mud-cracked earth will always be there. *Not yet. There will be time to create.* The sinking in his stomach grew as the road he watched grew longer, too. The road at his back in the rear view mirror came into view. And so did the thought to which Francis had known all along. So he set off; left there, the great Artificers, faint and vanishing as a mirage on the hot black road. To his back, over arid plains, clashed an unstoppable tempest brooding in the divinity of the distant sky. Away from it he'll drive; to a home with his scrape-razor on a basement bedside table. The rain will come when it comes; it cannot be sought, Francis knew, as he began to drive through sun and sky and light and air. Off to be now a sensible man; though by and by a fool; presently at peace.

ML